INNOCENT UNTIL PROVEN FAE

THE PARANORMAL PI FILES - BOOK FIVE

JENNA WOLFHART

This book was produced in the UK using British English, and the setting is London. Some spelling and word usage may differ from US English.

Innocent Until Proven Fae

Book Five in The Paranormal PI Files

Cover Design by Covers by Juan

Copyright © 2019 by Jenna Wolfhart

All rights reserved.

No part of this book may be reproduced in any form or by any electronic or mechanical means, including information storage and retrieval systems, without written permission from the author, except for the use of brief quotations in a book review.

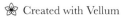

ALSO BY JENNA WOLFHART

The Paranormal PI Files

Live Fae or Die Trying

Dead Fae Walking

Bad Fae Rising

One Fae in the Grave

Innocent Until Proven Fae

All's Fae in Love and War (Coming Soon!)

The Bone Coven Chronicles

Witch's Curse

Witch's Storm

Witch's Blade

Witch's Fury

Protectors of Magic

Wings of Stone

Carved in Stone

Bound by Stone

Shadows of Stone

Order of the Fallen

Ruinous

Nebulous

Ravenous (Coming Soon!)

Otherworld Academy

A Dance with Darkness

A Song of Shadows

A Touch of Starlight

Dark Fae Academy

A Cage of Moonlight

A Heart of Midnight

A Throne of Illusions (Coming Soon!)

1

The flickering candles cast ominous shadows on the windowless walls. I sat in the far back corner of Gordon's Wine Bar without a single weapon to keep me company. After the fight that had broken out in these caverns a couple of months ago, the owner had a strict "no supes with weapons" policy, highlighted by the half a dozen signs clinging to the walls.

I didn't blame him, but I felt pretty damn naked without my steel.

It was a quiet night at Gordon's. There were a handful of humans clustered around the small wooden tables, but the crowd was thin. Humans avoided anywhere even remotely supe-related these days. They no longer found us intriguing curiosities to gawk at. Now, we were dangerous, violent psychopaths who were destroying their city.

Again, I didn't blame them. Nemain had launched a series of deadly attacks against London when she'd had her eyes set on Balor's throne. In the end, she'd gotten it.

But it wouldn't last long. Not if I had anything to say about it.

A very familiar face poked around the corner of the back section of the bar, her pixie-cut brunette hair framing her face. She licked her lips, flicked her eyes from one end of the bar to the other, and then settled her gaze on me.

I lifted my hand and gave her a small wave. "Hey, Ondine."

She cast a glance over her shoulder, her sunken cheeks highlighted by the shadows, and then she scurried on over to me. With a sigh, she plopped down in the chair and leaned forward on elbows that dug into the table. "You really shouldn't have called me here. Nemain will hang anyone who she thinks will stand against her."

"And yet you came," I said quietly.

She puffed out a sigh and leaned back in her chair. "How's Kyle? Is he okay?"

My lips twitched with a smile. "He's fine. You don't need to worry about Kyle. Or the cactus you gave him. It's still alive, by the way. On the other hand, he's incredibly worried about you."

Red bloomed in Ondine's cheeks. "Where is he? In London still?"

I sighed, leaned back in my chair, and shook my head. "That I can't tell you."

Ondine winced. "Oh, come on, Clark. You know I would never tell Nemain a thing."

"It's not you I worry about. It's her. She can force you to do whatever she wants. That includes giving up information about Kyle and the others. And you know it." I gave her a sad smile. "It's not a risk I'm willing to take. I'm sorry."

Her eyelids fluttered shut, and she sighed. "I hate her so much, Clark."

"I know."

"But despite all that, you know I can't tell you a damn thing," she said through gritted teeth. "She has been extremely...*thorough* with the orders she's given all of us. Not to mention, I don't even know all that much. It's not like she's waxing poetic about her evil plans to a lowly subject like me."

"That's why I called several of you here," I said.

Ondine's eyes widened when two more of our fellow Crimson Court fae joined the table. Ondine was the only one I knew particularly well. I'd also invited Emma, a notorious gossip who no doubt had her ear on the ground at Court. I had no reason to trust her, other than a gut feeling that she'd hate Nemain's reign just as much as anyone else. I'd also asked for a fae named Oscar. I'd only known of him through Cormac and Duncan, two powerful warriors that we'd lost in the war so far. He had stubbornly refused to flee the House when Nemain's Fianna had descended upon it, hoping he could stay and find a way to destroy her from the inside out.

He hadn't counted on her all-encompassing orders. Oscar hadn't been able to do a damn thing. Until now.

"Don't just stand there," I said with a wave of my hand. "Come on and sit down. I'm not going to bite."

Oscar yanked back a chair and lowered his thin, lithe frame into it. Unlike Cormac and Duncan, he was as skinny as a pole. He had long fingers and a jawline that could cut like steel. Something about him screamed otherworldly creature, a fact that was amplified by his blue-tinted hair.

Emma carefully sat down beside him, placing her clasped hands in her lap. "We should make this quick. The Fianna are..." She flicked her eyes back and forth. "Everywhere."

"Well, they're not here." I pointed at the nearest sign. Not only did it specify no supes with weapons, but it had big bold lettering that said, 'NO FAERIES' at the top. "Not allowed."

Emma leaned forward and hissed, "But we're faeries."

"I made a deal with the owner. We're allowed to meet here, as long as we don't bring in any weapons or cause any fights. So, we need to be as inconspicuous as possible." I tossed Oscar a cowboy hat. "Best cover up that hair of yours."

He let out a grunt, but he didn't argue. Instead, he slammed the hat over his head and peered out at us from beneath the wide brim. A few blueish strands still peeked out around the edges, but it was good enough for now.

"So, what's this all about?" he asked. "'Cause I gotta be honest. I've tried everything. There's no way around the bond. Hell, even saying that is dancing super close to the edge of what we can and can't do."

"You let me worry about that," I said, opting for caution. If Nemain somehow discovered we'd had a meeting, I wanted them to have as little information as possible to give to her. "First things first...how is Elise?"

A pang went through my heart just at the mention of my friend. She'd been unable to get out of the Court in time. Much like Oscar, she had stayed behind, taking her duties as Balor's second-in-command as seriously as she could. She wanted to ensure that every single fae got to safety before she left herself.

I hadn't heard a single word about her since.

I was scared as hell what that might mean.

Ondine ground her teeth together and shook her head. "Can't say. That's off-limits info, Clark."

I pressed my lips together. That wasn't a good sign. If Nemain was purposely keeping information about Elise a secret, then that meant there was something she needed to hide. With a deep breath, I closed my eyes and called upon my mind-reading powers. The fae of the Crimson Court might not be able to tell me what was going on under Nemain's cruel reign, but they didn't have to. All I had to do was poke around inside their minds.

I tried Ondine first. Out of the three of them, she was the most likely to know what Elise had been up to. She, Moira, Ondine, and I were all friends, and if anyone was looking out for Elise, it would be her.

Ondine's mind was easy to enter. She seemed to sense what I was doing, and she opened herself up to being read.

I haven't seen Elise since Nemain sat down on the throne. She's taken her somewhere, but I don't know where.

Tears stung my eyes as I pulled myself out of Ondine's head. She met my gaze head on, her eyes full of sadness. Slowly, she gave a nod.

Emma leaned forward and hissed, "What the hell just happened? What are you doing?"

Oscar crossed his arms over his chest and leaned back in the chair. "I see what Clark's plan is. She's going to read our minds to get the information she wants. Not a bad idea."

Emma's eyes practically bugged out of her head. "Uh uh. That's complete bollocks. I don't want you digging around in my head."

Oscar cut his eyes toward Emma. "Why? Something you hiding, love?"

Her cheeks flamed. "No, of course not. It's just… look, I don't like the idea of someone else reading my mind. Is that so weird?"

"No, it's pretty normal." I glanced from Ondine to Oscar and back to Emma. Maybe Oscar had a point. Sure, most people hated having their minds read, but this wasn't a normal situation. If I were in Emma's position, I'd be chomping at the bits, excited that we'd found a loophole around Nemain's orders.

But she wasn't excited. Hell, she looked scared.

"She knows something," I said to Oscar.

He gave a solemn nod, and Ondine pressed her lips together.

With another deep breath, I plunged forward. This time, I felt some resistance. Emma was practically screaming inside of her head, doing everything she could to block me out. I ground my teeth together, forcing myself to focus around all the noise. Somewhere underneath it all, I would find what I'd come here looking for.

I pushed inside a bit further, past the screeching.

I don't want Clark to find out that I'm helping Nemain. I

don't want her to know that I've helped put Elise in the dungeons. She'll hate me. Not that I should care. Clark is a half-blood. She's not even fully one of us. We're all doomed if she's the only one who can help us.

I'd heard enough. I pulled back out of Emma's head and gave her a frank look. Her eyes were cast down toward the ground, her cheeks a deep shade of red. "I'm sorry."

"Look." I placed my palms flat on the table and leaned forward. "I know I'm not anyone's top pick for saving the Court. I'm new. I'm half-shifter. And I'm not even an official member anymore." Which was the only way I'd been able to meet with them in the first place. "But I'm all you've got."

Nemain had given the fae of House Beimnech—now called House Nemain—several standing orders. The first, no contact with any member of the previous House Beimnech who fled, and no contact with Balor himself either. What Nemain had failed to realise was that Balor had never officially re-inducted me back into his House. So, they could talk to me. Kind of. There was also the pesky rule of sharing no information with any outsider at all.

They could talk to me. They just couldn't tell me anything important.

"Duncan seemed to have faith in you," Oscar said with a slow nod. "And if he did, then so can we. Even if you are a banished half-fae who helped Nemain once upon a time."

"Helped her, under extreme duress," I added through clenched teeth, "when I was just a kid. My step-father—"

Oscar held up a hand, interrupting me. "He

manipulated you. I know. I wouldn't be here if I really thought you had anything to do with all of that."

My cheeks warmed. "Good. Then, you need to let me read your mind. I know it sucks. I know it feels like an invasion of your privacy. But this is the only way for me—and Balor—to find out what you know."

Oscar let out a long, slow exhale. He twisted toward Emma whose lips were pressed tightly together. She still stared hard at the table, twin dots of pink on her cheeks. "I know some stuff. We all do. But it's not much."

"Not much is better than nothing," I replied.

Slowly, he gave a nod. "Go on, love."

Thank the seven. As willing as I was to dig around in Oscar's brain for the sake of the realm—hell, for the sake of the whole world at this point—I'd always hated using my power as an interrogation technique, against people's wishes. It didn't feel right, forcing myself into their heads.

I closed my eyes once again, this time focusing on Oscar's mind. He welcomed me inside with open arms, and there were no barriers to stop me from delving straight into his thoughts. Snippets of conversations and random phrases swirled around me, but then they stopped suddenly, as if someone had just pressed the 'mute' button on the remote control to his brain.

Clark….try….talk to you.

Hmm, that was interesting. Since my time joining the Court, only a few fae had been able to communicate directly to my mind from theirs. Fionn, Balor, and now Oscar, though his words were filled with static, as if he were trying to speak to me over a long distance.

I can hear you, I thought back to him. *What do you know about Nemain?*

She's planning something…to take…the Ivory Court.

My heart thumped hard. *What are you saying? Nemain is going to take control of the Ivory Court? When? How?*

Moving fast. Three Courts…not two.

With a deep breath, I pulled myself out of Oscar's head, my heart rocketing around my chest like a pinball stuck in a machine. This was bad. This was *really* bad. We'd known that Nemain would go after another Court *eventually*, but we hadn't expected it to happen so soon.

Nemain wanted to gain more power so she could control all of Faerie. And, if we didn't stop her, she would get it.

2

I felt him before I saw him. Despite the fact his throne had been stolen from him, Balor's power was just as potent as it had ever been—maybe even more so. Now, he had no outlet for his strength; nothing to command or control. Wisps of his magic curled around me as he approached from behind. Heat sparked deep within my core, my entire body humming from his distant touch.

He rounded the table and sunk into the seat across from me, where Ondine had been only a few moments before. In the past couple of weeks, the dark stubble on Balor's jaw had lengthened, and the silver streaks through his hair had multiplied.

It made him seem a bit wild, rugged, and raw, a look that I found next to impossible to resist.

Not that I'd ever really been able to resist the former Prince. I'd wanted him from the moment I first saw him.

He leaned back in the chair, the wood creaking

underneath his muscular weight. "Tell me what you've learned."

He raised an eyebrow over the black patch he still wore at all times. But, instead of it protecting the world from his powerful flames, it now hid the black charred stone that had replaced the bright orange iris.

"You're not going to be happy," I said, tapping a single finger on the table.

A hollow sigh escaped from his throat. "At least tell me they're okay."

"They're fine," I said. "For the most part. Emma seems pretty torn up about the whole thing, and Nemain is making her do things she doesn't want to do. Pretty much what we expected."

He closed his eye, nostrils flaring. "I hate this. I despise being unable to be in the same room with my fae. This is my worst nightmare, come to life right before my eyes, and there is nothing I can do to stop it."

"Balor." I leaned forward and slid my hand on top of his. Instantly, sparks of magic shot up my arm. My breath got caught in my throat as I stared at the spot where our skin touched. Things like this kept happening between us, now that we'd agreed to stop putting walls up between us. It was like a dam had burst, the true power of our mating bond crashing down around us.

Balor dragged his eyes away from our hands and met my gaze. The depths of his emotions almost knocked me right off my chair. What were we talking about again?

"Tell me what you've learned," he said, voice sounding strained.

I sucked a deep breath in through my nose. "Elise has been taken to the dungeons, and Nemain plans to take control of another Court next. The Ivory Court."

Balor's back snapped straight. "Already? But she's only just established herself on my crimson throne."

"Apparently, she wants to make a move before anyone has a chance to get organised against her. She's afraid some of the Courts will band together. Two out of the seven courts against five doesn't give her great odds. But three against four? That could be a winnable war, if she's smart."

Balor scowled, bracing his arms on the table that squatted between us. "Nemain is much smarter than I've given her credit for, likely from her years spent watching and learning the politics of the Courts. Has anyone ever told you her story?"

I gave a quick shake of my head. "And I've never asked. After what happened with my parents, I always figured the less I knew about her, the better. It was easier to write her out of my mind that way." And keep my secrets hidden.

It was a relief not to have to worry about that anymore.

"Nemain is old," Balor began, leaning closer. "Older than me. Centuries ago, she was the sixth daughter of a solitary fae. She had no claims to anything. She had no protection from any Court. Her eldest brother got killed, trying to take control of some lands." Balor sighed and shook his head. "Despite all that, she somehow worked her way up the ladder of power. She started out as a squire. Then, she became a knight, a warrior in one of our many wars. After that, she kept working her way up to the top, higher and higher until she claimed my sister's Court."

My heart thumped hard in my chest. I had dreamt of Nemain as a warrior. She had manipulated the Morrigan into leaving her army behind. But that had been just a dream and nothing more. It was impossible for it to have been anything else. I must have heard this story somewhere before, and it had eked its way into my subconscious.

Balor frowned, reading—and most likely scenting—the change in my mood immediately. "Is there something wrong?"

I tapped my finger against the table and desperately wished I'd ordered myself another gin and tonic. I hadn't told Balor about my dream. Didn't think it was necessary, really. And, I didn't really want to tell him now either. I knew what he'd say, what he'd think. Hell, he already thought it.

But I was not the reincarnation of the Morrigan. It was impossible.

Still…I'd made a promise to myself and to Balor. No more secrets. Keeping things from him had caused enough strife between us.

"I had a dream about Nemain. She was a warrior in it," I said with a shrug. "Just a coincidence, I'm sure."

Balor's eyebrows winged upwards. "We need to get you to Caer. She'll have answers."

I let out a heavy sigh and shook my head. "You want to ask her if I'm the Morrigan. Well, we don't need to trek all the way out to the Lake of the Dragon's Mouth to know the answer to that."

Balor pursed his lips, his single red eye glittering with the light of the candles. "We will go see her. And you should prepare yourself, Clark. Perhaps you aren't the Morrigan. But you are *something*. The answers you find there might be ones you don't want to hear, but you still need to hear them."

I pressed up from the table. Enough about the Morrigan and Nemain's past as a warrior. What happened centuries ago didn't matter. We needed a plan on how to deal with what was happening *now* before Nemain got control of another Court and it was too damn late for us to do a thing.

Out of the corner of my eye, something flashed. Frowning, I turned to stare down the underground tunnels of Gordon's, hoping against hope that the fae hadn't wandered back down here to speak to me about something. If they came face-to-face with Balor, they would no doubt be forced to tell their new Queen about it.

But it wasn't Ondine, or Oscar, or Emma who had caught my eye. It was a small hooded figure, whose face was obscured by the thick black material curtaining her face. I frowned as she—or he—scurried away from us and toward the exit, feeling the slight hint of magic wafting toward us.

"We have company," I said, pushing away from the table. Balor quickly followed behind me as we pushed out of the bar and into the streets. Outside, everything was dark, quiet, and eerily calm. Around Bank, the streets usually pulsed with energy, especially at night.

Not a single soul was anywhere to be seen.

Chills swept along my arms, and a strange prickling sensation raised all the hair on the back on my neck. Something was wrong. We were being watched.

I'd felt this sensation once before, when I'd flown across the sea in search of Nemain. That time, I'd been right. She had been there, watching us every step of the way, luring us into a trap.

"Nemain is nearby," I said to Balor, as quietly as I could. "Or, at least, someone is."

"Good."

I frowned at him, ignoring the sweat that was gathering on my palms. Due to the nature of the whole Gordon's Wine Bar weapon situation, neither of us had our swords. Not ideal if we were about to face Nemain and her warriors.

Some humans suddenly stumbled out from a nearby door that emptied into the alley. They were laughing, leaning on each other as they grasped their cigarette packs in their hands. The laughter died on their lips when they spotted me and Balor. Anger and fear hardened their eyes.

If it had been just me, they likely wouldn't have taken any notice. With my shorter stature and my very non-ethereal face, I could blend in with humanity pretty well.

Balor stood the hell out though. His tall and commanding presence radiated with pure, unadulterated power. Magic hummed along his skin. Fae-like pointy ears poked through his dark, silver-streaked hair. And his single visible eye. That flaming red eye. It could pierce into souls.

So, yeah. They knew we were fae.

INNOCENT UNTIL PROVEN FAE

"Call the police," one of the humans hissed to the other. He was tall and lanky, like a basketball player in the states, but he was still nothing compared to Balor's intimidating height.

"That would be a bad idea." Balor took a step toward the humans, flexing his abundant muscles. I'd never seen Balor go after a human before. I doubt he would now. But they didn't need to know that.

"See," the other human said, muttering beneath his breath through a thick wiry beard. With his horned-rimmed glasses and his perfectly-fitted plaid shirt, I bet I could give him some kombucha and he'd happily go on his merry way. "I told you the fae were dangerous."

I rolled my eyes at Balor's flexing. "Look, we're not dangerous, and we're not going to hurt you. But, we are in the middle of something, and it's probably for the best if you go back inside. Yeah?"

The bearded one frowned. "In the middle of something in an alley? Yeah, that's not suspicious at all."

"We're..." I wet my lips, glanced at Balor, and then placed a palm on his chest. "You know. *Busy.*"

God, this was embarrassing, but I really needed them to go away without calling the cops. Any second now, Nemain and her Fianna would descend upon this alley. I didn't want any humans to get caught in the crossfire.

Tall and Lanky sneered, glancing from me to Balor and then back again. "What are you, some kind of whore for fae wankers?"

Balor's power pulsed, though his expression didn't

change. He took one step closer to the humans. Gritting my teeth, I pressed harder against his chest. "That's none of your damn business. Now, can you go back inside?"

They both stared hard, their hands crunching their cigarette packs. They were definitely considering *not* listening to me and staying here instead. That prickle on the back of my neck only intensified, the warning that Nemain and her warriors were near.

"Fuck it," I muttered to myself before turning toward Balor and pressing up onto my toes. I wrapped my arms around his neck and pulled his lips to mine. Our mouths crashed together, and the heat of his body enveloped mine. Sparks danced along every inch of my skin. For a moment, I forgot about everything else. The humans weren't there, watching us. Nemain and her army were back up north. The city was at peace.

And Balor and I were together, just as we'd always been and how we always would be.

Laughter broke through the moment. I gasped and pulled back, heat filling my cheeks.

"Alright, alright," the bearded one said, grinning as he took a step back toward the door of the building. "We'll leave you to it. Guess even fae have needs, eh?"

Finally, they both disappeared from the alley.

Balor glanced down at me, eyebrows winging upward. "I'm not sure you needed to be so convincing, Clark. You were practically purring."

"Oh, stop gloating." I swatted at him. "It got rid of them, didn't it?"

"Oh yes," another voice said, breaking through the

silence of the night. Several forms shifted out of the shadows. Fianna. All with swords that glinted off the light of the street lamps. "But you're not going to get rid of *us* that easily."

3

*B*alor shifted his body in front of mine, a darker shade of his power now pulsing from his skin. When he spoke, his voice was a growl. "I have to say, I'm surprised to see you here. I was under the impression that Nemain forbade you from being within ten meters of me."

"The Fianna are exempt from that law. And for good reason." Aed stepped forward from his warriors, the bulk of his body just as wide as Balor's. His thick beard and bushy eyebrows had grown since I'd last seen him, and he looked more like a bear than a fae.

"Law?" Balor chuckled, but there was no sign of laughter on his face. "So, not only has she dubbed herself Queen but she is also acting as though she has the authority to make laws. Interesting that you would follow someone who spins power from nothing."

"That is exactly why we follow her." Aed motioned to the warriors behind him. They all shifted further out of the shadows, filling the quiet spaces of the alley. There were about ten in total. Balor and I were way outnumbered. And worse, we didn't have our weapons.

"You're seriously suggesting that you follow someone because she likes to pretend she has power that she doesn't actually have?" Truth was, I couldn't care less about the reasons Aed and his fellow warriors had decided to follow a murderous psychopath. I just figured I would keep him talking for as long as possible, to give Balor a chance to come up with a plan.

I was fresh out of ideas myself.

Aed chuckled and lifted one of his furry brows. It wiggled as it moved, like a caterpillar. "Ain't you doing the same with Balor now, love? Tell me, where does his power come from now? Nemain took his Court away from him, and his fiery eye is nowhere to be seen." He chuckled again. "Get it? Eye. Seen."

"I mean, the fact you think that's funny kind of explains how you'd be dumb enough to follow Nemain." I let out my own sarcastic chuckle, flicking my gaze to Balor. His face had turned a darker shade of red, and the magic of his power was practically bouncing off of him now. Aed had hit a nerve. A very raw nerve.

Balor was about to blow.

"You chose the wrong ruler, Aed," Balor said, voice rumbling from his throat. "And when I return to my throne, I will not forget it."

"It's cute that you think you'll ever get anywhere near your crimson skulls again." Aed punched one fist into his open palm. "Especially since you'll be dying here tonight."

So, I guessed my whole distraction technique hadn't worked. Time to try something else. Like…

running? That sounded like a good option right about now.

I wrapped my hand around Balor's arm and squeezed tight, pulling him back from the Fianna. But he was like an immovable stone. Rock hard and stubborn as hell. He whipped toward me, frowned. Obviously, the pesky fact about us not having weapons wasn't going to stop him from jumping into this fight.

"Can we have a little chat?" I asked as softly as I could. "Maybe, I don't know, somewhere private?"

"Your little seduction tricks aren't going to work on us, Clark," Aed cut in with another punch against his palm. "You won't be able to run us off like you did those humans."

Balor rolled his shoulders back. "I welcome the fight."

Aed's hand found the hilt of his sword. He pulled it from the silver sheath strapped to his side, and the singing of steel filled the city night. The blade flashed in the darkness, so sharp it could cut through stone.

My hand reached for my own hilt instinctively, but it came up empty. Damn Gordon's Wine Bar and their damn rules. If they hadn't outlawed weapons, we wouldn't be caught out unarmed like this.

Instead, my fists would have to do. I bounced on the balls on my feet, curling my fingers tightly together.

"Clark," Balor gave a warning. But what the hell did he expect me to do?

Aed swung his sword at my head. I ducked down and hopped out of the way, rolling back my shoulders as he paused, eyes wide. "You're a lot faster than a half-shifter should be."

JENNA WOLFHART

"I've been practicing." I shot him a grin. "And just wait until you see what my friends can do."

The ravens were already circling overhead, screaming out in rage at the attack. Any moment now and they would swoop down to join the fight, though my heart squeezed a little tighter at the thought. These Fianna were highly-trained and carrying some serious steel. I didn't want any of my birds to get hurt.

Aed seemed to sense my hesitation, and shot me his own grin in response. "They're welcome to try."

He raised a hand, flicked his fingers at the half-dozen Fianna behind him. They all sprang forward. Balor let out a growl and punched Aed right in the throat. The sword clattered onto the concrete, one second before Balor's hand closed around the hilt.

He got the blade up just in time to slam it against Aed's second weapon.

"Call the cops, mate. We can't wait any longer."

The voice that had spoken had been so quiet that I wasn't totally sure I'd heard it at first. It was almost as though it had come from deep inside a well or from ten miles away. No one else seemed to notice. The fight raged on.

Slowly, I turned to face the noise. Down the alley, I *felt* rather than saw two forms huddled behind a stack of wooden crates. Somehow, I just knew it was the same two humans that Balor and I had run into before.

They'd come back. And they'd stumbled straight into the middle of the fight.

"I thought I heard something," Aed's deep voice rumbled as he rushed down the alley toward the humans. "Brought some back up, did you?"

"No!" I shouted and threw up a hand, stumbling after him. My heart pounded hard against my ribcage, horror rocking through me. If he found the humans calling the cops, he would not hesitate to kill them.

The two men, The Bearded One and Tall and Lanky suddenly sprang up from their hiding place and began to back down the alley with their hands raised before them. Several more humans filtered out of the door, and the glint of steel sang through the night. I swallowed hard, pausing in my steps. Some of the humans even had guns.

"Shit," I murmured as Balor stepped up beside me. The Fianna had all turned their attention on the humans, the fight with us seemingly forgotten. There were not many things that could cause instant death in a fae. A good strong sword struck in the right place was one of them.

Another was a gun.

"You need to leave," one of the humans called out, lifting a long-barrelled shotgun to his shoulder. "We've called the cops. They're on the way."

I took one look at Balor, torn. He was already on the outs with the human authorities. We couldn't risk getting caught here in a fight with another fae. But we couldn't very well leave the Fianna here alone with the humans. These two men were playing with a fire that couldn't be controlled.

Aed frowned and slid his sword back into the sheath, taking a wide step away from the humans. He held up his hands. "We will go. Willingly. Let it be known that Nemain, the Queen of Faerie, wishes no harm on the humans of this city. She has ordered us to stand down against any and all non-magical beings. This is us standing down. Tell your friends."

Aed turned and shot Balor a wicked smile. My heart thumped. I understood what he was doing. And while I was relieved he wasn't going to drive his sword through an innocent's chest, I knew it was all for show. Nemain wanted to get the humans of the city on her side. Unfortunately for us, it was working.

"Come on, Clark," Balor said, his lip curling. "Let's go."

4

Our base of operations was the one place in the world I never would have guessed until Balor had chosen it: my old flat. On the plus side, Nemain would never think to look for us here. On the negative side…well, I had run into my old landlord more often than not, and the awkwardness made me feel like crawling into a hole and never coming out.

"Clark," Henry said as Balor and I headed straight toward the dingy flight of stairs, wobbling as he inched down the hall. "You look like you're in a hurry. No trouble, remember, love?"

Yes, yes. That was the whole deal, one that Balor had managed to wrangle somehow. After we'd come back to London without a place to call home, Balor had filled me in on a little secret that he'd been keeping. All this time, he'd kept ahold of my flat, paying the landlord twice what the tiny East London place was worth. He'd wanted me to have somewhere "just in case" things went sideways, especially after he'd banished me. And just in case things didn't work out with Ronan.

Things hadn't worked out with Ronan.

Ronan who, I might add, hadn't been in touch since he'd fled the city along with the rest of the Pack.

"No trouble at all." I gave Henry a too-bright smile. "We are just minding our own business. I don't take on cases anymore, remember?"

He let out a grumble. "Been a long time since you released a new podcast episode."

Huh. I smiled. "Didn't know you were a fan of the Paranormal PI Files."

"Would hardly call myself a fan." He grunted again. "I only listened to make sure you weren't causing trouble for the rest of the building. But you know." He lowered his voice, edged in close. "I'm sure all your *actual* listeners would love to hear your take on all the…recent developments. The new, er, power in town."

He winced as he glanced at Balor. Humans knew all about the shift of power and the changes in the supernatural society. It had been all over the news. Television and radio stations had blasted constant updates about it in the days following, and memes had flared through the internet like wildfire. The story had been impossible to contain.

To be totally honest, a part of me wished I'd been on the scene myself. My podcasting had become a moneymaker for me, but it had started out as fun. I enjoyed speaking into the microphone, weaving tales and sharing my stories. But my hobby-turned-profession had taken a backseat to Crimson Court drama, pretty much from day one. Part of it was down to just

INNOCENT UNTIL PROVEN FAE

not having the time. But the other part? Hell, I couldn't even share most of what happened. Telling the world about our plots and our plans was too great a risk.

"Maybe when all of this is over, I'll do a whole series on it." I patted his arm. "We've got to win first though."

He gave a solemn nod. Unlike most of the rest of London, my old landlord seemed to be on our side. He didn't like the way Nemain had stolen the crown, and he wanted to see the city return to peace. So, he hadn't snitched. For that, I would be eternally grateful.

~

*U*pstairs, neither Moira or Kyle were anywhere to be seen. They'd left a curled piece of paper taped to the fridge that told us they'd gone to grab some takeaway for dinner. My stomach grumbled at the thought. I could really put away a big pile of sweet and sour Chinese right about now.

Fighting always made me hungry.

Balor carefully shut the door behind us and slid the five deadbolts into place. Since moving back into the flat, he'd gone all out with security. Cameras had been mounted just outside the door, down the stairs, and outside the front of the building. No one was getting in without us knowing about it.

After testing the locks a second time, Balor stalked to the small bank of computers we'd set up in the living room. Normally, Kyle sat behind them, keeping an eye on things. Balor clicked a few buttons, rewound the security footage, and audibly sighed when it didn't show anything but the normal comings and goings of the humans in this building.

No vampires, no shifters, and most importantly, no Nemain.

"If Nemain knew about this place, she would have attacked by now," I said, perching on the table. "She'd feel a lot better about her place as Queen if we were out of the picture."

"You may be right, Clark, but we can never relax. Not until this is over."

The silence rose up around us, almost deafening. It was so calm and still inside the flat, the total opposite of the blur of activity it had been this past week. We'd been going at full speed ever since we'd moved in, working ourselves into the ground to come up with a plan to take down Nemain.

I wet my lips, suddenly very aware of how close Balor was to me. "We're alone. For once."

We'd had no privacy, not with the four of us crammed into a tiny one-bedroom flat. To make things fair, we'd come up with a rota, each taking the single bed while the rest of us shared the living room where three inflatable mattresses were pushed up against one wall. When it had been Balor's night in the bed, I'd laid awake, thinking, wondering if I should go to him.

In the end, I hadn't, though every single part of me wished I had.

Balor's eyes flashed as he drank me in. "When we get the House back, I want you to move into my penthouse with me, Clark. Then, we can have as much time alone together as we want."

A thrill went through me at the thought. Me, living

with Balor Beimnech. Waking up in his arms every morning. Falling asleep wrapped together beneath the sheets. Heat poured through my neck, fingers of it reaching up to my ears.

With a smile, I stepped closer and pressed my hands against his chest. His muscles tensed beneath my fingers, making my breath catch. I breathed him in, filling up my head with the intoxicating scent of rich leather and smoky mist.

"Is that a yes?" he murmured as he slipped his thumb underneath my chin. He tipped back my head, drinking me in with a hunger and a need that was reflected deep within my core.

"I would like nothing more," I whispered, though that wasn't the full truth. There were many things I wanted just as much as, if not more. I wanted us to fully join together, after so many hours spent holding back and anticipating. I wanted to know what it felt like to let the mating magic consume me. I wanted Balor back on the throne, so we could focus on the fae, on our lives together, and on the future instead of the past.

But I also very much wanted to live with Balor.

Balor's mouth crushed mine. He wrapped his hand around the back of my head and dug his fingers into my mess of red hair. I moaned against him as pleasure curled through my gut, gripping his shirt tight in my fisted hands. Magic curled around me like a dozen soft fingers. It caressed my skin, my hair, my cheeks. The power of our bond snapped tight, and my body pressed up closer to Balor, instinctively.

My Prince pulled back suddenly, but he kept his forehead pressed hotly to mine. "We're alone."

"Yes," I whispered, gazing up at him. "I know."

He lifted me from the ground, his hands sliding around my thighs. I hooked my legs around his waist as he carried me out of the living room. We reached the bedroom door, kicked it open, and then slammed it shut behind us. All the while my heart raced in my chest, and my palms were slick from the intense need that had turned my entire body as hot as the sun.

More gently than I expected, Balor lowered me onto the mattress. The sheets were still thick with the scent of him, a tantalising combination of mist, leather, and wood. It sparked another wave of need, one that crashed over me so hard that I could barely breathe.

His hands snagged on my shirt and pulled the material over my head, exposing my peaked breasts to his eager lips. Desire ripped through me as he teased my nipples with his tongue. I arched my back toward him, desperate for more.

Balor responded eagerly. His mouth and hands made quick work of my breasts, and I was a writhing, needy mess beneath him. Slowly, he pushed off me and pulled his shirt over his head, revealing the hard planes of muscles I was desperate to touch.

I reached up and traced the lines of his abs, mesmerised by his perfectly-sculpted form.

He was beautiful. So beautiful it hurt.

My trousers came next, and then his. There was now no longer anything standing between us. My heart was a raging bonfire in my chest, my entire face flushed with heat. We had danced so close to this edge, numerous times. We'd never stepped past it, always pulling back before we took it too far.

But I was ready to give myself to him now, ready to finally seal our mating bond.

"Are you certain you want this, Clark?" he asked as he held his body over mine.

My heart thumped once, and then I nodded. "I've never wanted anything more."

Curls of powerful magic caressed my skin as Balor gently spread my legs with his knees. A rush of his magic filled me, just as he slowly pressed his length into my core. I gasped, eyes widening at the hardness of him. Stars danced in my eyes, pinpricks of light that were reflected in the reddening of his eye.

I reached up and pushed the eye patch away from his head. He paused, just for a moment, as I fully took him in, blackened eye and all. My hand slipped down to his cheek, my heart so full I swore it might burst.

"I want you," I whispered. "*All* of you."

His red iris flared with heat. With a growl, he pushed further into me. I kept my gaze locked on his as he rocked against me, our noses grazing, our lips whispering against each other. He plunged deeper and harder until my head rang with the sound of him. A strange white hot magic tore through my body just as the heat of him made my core explode into a million tiny shards.

A part of my soul broke out of me then. It hurtled into Balor's skin. He held on tight as I cried out, welcoming in the part of him that broke free of his own heart.

We were bound now. Nothing could ever tear us apart.

5

The front door of the flat opened and shut, but Balor didn't even flinch. He kept his arms wrapped tight around me while trailing his finger up and down my back. Every single swoop of his touch felt like a caress that was more than just a touch, reaching into the very depths of my soul.

I snuggled into the crook of his elbow and sighed. Voices were murmuring outside of the bedroom door. Moira and Kyle were back. Soon, Balor and I would have to leave our cocoon and return to the world.

I just wanted one more minute…

Another hour.

Hell, a whole year.

In here, all of our troubles felt like distant memories. I could ignore them forever like this.

"How are you feeling?" Balor murmured against the top of my head. "No seed quickening in your belly, I hope?"

I shifted my head back so that I could gaze up at the strong line of his jaw. "I'm pretty sure I wouldn't be able to tell this quickly. Besides, I thought we figured out a loophole with the curse."

"The loophole where I do not return to my rightful place on that throne?" His eyes went dark. "I am not certain I like that loophole, Clark."

With a frown, I sat up and gazed down at him. "We don't have much of a choice. When we defeat her, you won't be able to take up the Princely bond again. The magic that protects her will see to that. You can lead the fae, just…not the same way you have in the past."

He let out a heavy sigh and pushed himself up from the bed. He stood before me, body corded in muscle. Even now, as naked and vulnerable as he was, he looked so damn powerful. No one could ever mistake him for anything other than a Prince.

He didn't need the magic to confirm it, to control them.

"I am not certain the prophecy makes that kind of distinction."

"Caer said that if you have a son, he will kill you and destroy the entire Court. But she mentioned the Princely bond. She mentioned the throne."

He pressed his lips tightly together. "You're close, but you're not quite there. I have repeated these words in my head for years upon years. Her words are exactly as follows: Balor, the great smiter, will have a son. Laughter and love will fill his life. When that son is grown, he will kill the Prince of the Crimson Court. And then the Court will be torn to shreds by all of his enemies." Balor paused. "Regardless of whether or not the bond still works, I will still be Prince, Clark. The best way to avoid the prophecy

INNOCENT UNTIL PROVEN FAE

being fulfilled is for us to be careful with our love-making."

He strode closer, wrapped his arms around my back, and pulled me up against his muscular chest. His dark gaze took me in, heat flickering within his iris. "That is good for you, yes?"

I sighed. Of course it was okay. This was what we had to do in order to be together. We needed to do whatever it took to make sure the prophecy never came true. But that didn't stop the strange prickling sensation on the back of my neck, like something wasn't quite right, that I was missing something.

"Yes, it's good for me." I smiled up at him. "All I want is you."

He kissed me then, slow and rough and full of a passion that made my toes curl against the bare hardwood floor. Sparks of desire lit up in me again. I wanted him with every fiber of my being, and if we had to spend the rest of our lives tiptoeing around the prophecy, then so be it.

A knock sounded on the door, and Moira's voice drifted through the thin walls. "Er, I hate to interrupt whatever the hell is going on in there, but there's a report on the news about some fae trouble near Bank. That have anything to do with you guys?"

With a sigh, I dragged myself away from Balor. "Unfortunately, yes. We'll be right out."

~

I threw on some clothes and padded out into the living room in my bare feet, Balor right on my heels. Moira and Kyle both gave us awkward-as-hell looks, but they didn't say a word about how this must look. My hair was mussed and cascading like a wild river around my shoulders. Balor's shirt was rumpled. And my cheeks sported bright red dots of heat.

Moira cleared her throat.

"We found out some things, and didn't find out some other things," I began, desperate for the awkward silence to be replaced with something else. Quickly, Balor and I filled our two companions in on what had happened.

"So, let me get this straight." Moira's expression went dark. "Nemain threw Elise in the dungeons. Sweet Elise who would never hurt a damn fly?"

"I'm afraid so," I said quietly.

"Not to mention the whole throne shite." Moira threw up her hands and began to pace from one end of the living room to the next. "We're well and truly fucked."

"I have an idea," Kyle said. "We need more allies."

"No shit, Sherlock." I fought the urge to roll my eyes. Kyle was one of the smartest fae I'd ever met, but sometimes he stated the obvious. "We're basically a team of four at this point. Everyone else has gotten the hell out of dodge. Not even the vampires want to get involved."

"Fae allies," Kyle said. "Those who have a stake in what happens to the Courts."

"Isn't that the problem?" Moira asked with a frown. "Nemain is gathering allies left and right."

Kyle pursed his lips. "I wouldn't say forcing fae to join you is a great way to retain loyal allies. We

INNOCENT UNTIL PROVEN FAE

need someone who wants to be on our side. Willingly."

"Who?" I propped my fisted hands on my hips. "One of the other Courts?"

"No, someone much closer to home." Kyle slid his eyes to Balor. "Maeve, the Master of House Driscoll. You're still in contact with her, yes?"

"If by 'in contact' you mean that I still have her hidden safely within the West Norwood Catacombs, then yes. Though I would hardly call her an ally in this situation. She is not in control of her own functions. She's a Sluagh."

Kyle tapped on the table, his brows pushed tightly together. "The way the curse works, the victim's heart stops beating momentarily. Technically, they are dead for a moment and then not, which is how the mind is numbed to be controlled by the strange Sluagh magic."

Balor frowned. "Yes, but I don't see where you're going with this, Kyle."

"Maeve's temporary death would have broken her bond with you. Technically, she is free. If we're somehow able to reverse the Sluagh spell, I doubt the bond could come into play again. She would need to be inducted again, just like Clark would."

Balor's eyes widened. "I see what you're saying. Maeve would be able to choose a side, without the interference of Nemain's bond."

Moira frowned. "What's to stop her from joining Nemain willingly? Then, we'll have given our enemy even more allies."

"I think that's a risk we have to take," Balor said quietly. "We could use her support. We could use her army. This could be the way we get the upper hand over Nemain."

"So, how are we going to do that?" I crossed my arms over my chest. While this was theoretically a good idea, the logistics weren't on our side. Right now, Maeve was nothing more than a member of the walking dead. On the plus side, we were the only ones who knew what had happened to the Master of House Driscoll, and we were the only ones who knew where she was. Except…Elise.

"We need to find a sorcerer willing to remove the magic of the Sluagh spell," Kyle said.

Lifting my brows, I nodded. "In the meantime, we need to move her and the others somewhere else. Elise knows where we're keeping them hidden. If Nemain realises that she knows something, she could force her to spill."

Balor nodded slowly. "You're right. The West Norwood Catacombs are no longer safe for the Sluagh. We'll need to find another underground den for them to stay while we hunt down a cure."

Kyle took up his station behind the bank of computers, his hands poised above the stainless steel keyboard. When we'd hastily removed everyone from the House, Kyle had refused to leave without his trusty keyboard, the only possession he'd brought with him. Apparently, it was better than a normal keyboard, but it just looked like a chunk of metal to me.

He tapped around for a few minutes, his screen whirring from one thing to the next so fast that it was impossible to keep up with. "Kyle, what exactly *is* your power, anyway?"

I couldn't believe I'd never asked before, but the

INNOCENT UNTIL PROVEN FAE

conversation had never come up. He'd always been so focused on his screens that I'd almost forgotten he would have a magical gift to go along with his techie mind.

"My brain consumes information faster than a typical brain," he muttered, almost too low for me to hear. "I thought you had realised that when I found things so quickly for you."

Huh. It made sense. No wonder he spent most of his time in front of a screen.

"Nice power," I said with a nod before turning to Moira.

She grinned. "Mine's fighting. I am exceptionally skilled with the blade."

"Among other weapons," Balor added. "Kyle, tell me what you've found."

Kyle's tapping had stopped. He was peering at the screen through his mop of red hair with his tongue stuck out between his lips. "Well, you're going to think this sounds mad, but a sorcerer has been putting up ads on social media for a couple of weeks. 'Sorcerer for hire' and that kind of thing."

Balor braced his hand on the desk and leaned forward to stare at the screen. I couldn't help but notice the way his arms rippled, arms that had been around me only moments ago. "He's trying to sell himself and his powers. Humans are probably going wild over this. Do you think you can find his contact details?"

Kyle nodded and pulled up an email address from the sorcerer's website. He shot off a note, while keeping the details about us as anonymous as possible.

And then, we all waited, glancing around at each other with question marks in our eyes.

"What now?" I asked.

Ding.

The computer chimed almost instantaneously.

"That was fast," Balor and I said, in unison.

Kyle quickly cracked open the reply. "He says he'd be more than happy to talk to us about our 'supernatural problem'. He gave us a time and a place to meet him." He glanced up, grinned. "Looks like we've found our man."

6

"The only problem is," Balor said, pacing from one end of the living-room-turned-command-station to the other, "the Sluagh need to be moved immediately. If Nemain has Elise held captive in the dungeons, it's only a matter of time before she starts demanding answers."

"If she hasn't already started." Moira's eyelids fluttered shut as she sucked a sharp breath in through her nose. "God, I hope Elise is okay."

I flicked my eyes to Balor. "What do you think of us breaking her out of there?"

Balor slipped his hands into his pockets and strode over to the window to peer out at the brilliant view of the brick wall next door. "I want nothing more than to extract Elise from the current situation. Unfortunately, I see no way of doing that without risking the liberation of every other fae in my House. We would likely get caught and be forced to fight for the Crimson Court right then and there."

"And there aren't enough of us to win," Kyle

muttered beneath his breath. "I wish you could have just brought Ondine back here after you met her in the bar. She's in so much danger, too."

I ground my teeth together and closed my eyes. Balor was right, as much as I hated it. Elise was stuck in a dungeon, having who-knew-what being done to her. Ondine was stuck in the Court, playing pretend and hoping she wouldn't get caught. It wasn't in my nature to hold back. The boiling fire within me wanted to storm in, guns blazing.

But Balor's fiery eye was gone. Moira was a great fighter, and I was learning fast. Kyle, on the other hand, didn't know the pointy end of a blade from the pommel. If we attacked Nemain now, we would not win.

"So, we just...leave her there," I said around a bitter lump of charcoal in my throat.

"It's only temporary," Balor said. "Once we have Maeve and her army behind us, we will take back the House."

I just had to pray to every deity that ever existed that Elise and Ondine would still be okay by then.

$\approx$

We waited until nightfall before making the trek to the West Norwood Catacombs. As necessary as the current mission was, I would not say that I was looking forward to returning to the underground crypts. The last time I'd been there, shit had really gone down. Tiarnan and I had been attacked by Sluagh, and we'd been forced to lock ourselves in a room with a bunch of corpses.

INNOCENT UNTIL PROVEN FAE

Like I said, fun times.

Thinking of Tiarnan, my heart squeezed tight. I couldn't believe that I'd trusted him, even knowing that he'd only recently been a part of Fionn's team. Fionn, the fae who had done everything in his power to rip Balor off his throne. Fionn, the fae who had wanted to execute me.

I shuddered as we scaled the cemetery gate. Balor caught the motion, probably smelled the unease on me. He gave me an encouraging smile.

"Don't worry. Maeve isn't like the other Sluagh you encountered here."

Somehow, I doubted that was the truth. Being fae, and a royal one at that, wouldn't stop her from succumbing to the darkest parts of the curse. Plus, if time made any difference at all, she had been a Sluagh for months.

Balor's eye flicked to where my hand rested stubbornly on the hilt of my sword. "When the sorcerer died, it left fae Sluagh without a master to control them. They merely wander through the catacombs now. There is nothing to fear."

"Then, why did you have Kyle stay back at base?" Moira pointed out with arched brows.

Balor gave her a pointed look, but didn't respond. Instead, he took the lead of our little trio of an army and led us through the twisty paths of the cemetery. As we wound deeper into the maze of crypts and tombstones, a strange, eerie silence filled the midnight air. Not a single bird fluttered between the dense trees, and the bulbous grey clouds obscured any moonlight that might fall at our feet. London's Magnificent Cemetery or not, it was bloody creepy.

I cleared my throat. "You know, I think I would have been more comfortable charging right into the middle of Nemain's army. This place is pure evil."

Moira grunted in agreement.

Soon, we stood clustered at the top of a crumbling set of stairs that descended into the catacombs. Tendrils of darkness clung to each step as they curved toward an arched doorway. The last time I'd been here, a black nothingness stood between the world and what was within. Now, a make-shift steel door had been affixed to the stone, creating a clash of old and new. I was assuming this was Balor's doing.

I kept my gaze focused forward, nerves tripping the veins in my neck. "If they are so harmless, why have you locked them inside?"

"I didn't want to give any nosy tourists the bright idea and have them wander inside. The catacombs are off-limits to the public, but that doesn't mean people don't sneak inside. Besides, it's for Maeve's protection more than anything. As soon as Sluagh step above ground, they begin to decompose."

Balor boldly strode down the steps and shoved a key into the lock. I inched down behind him, Moira by my side. Her face was as white as a sheet, her eyes as hard as steel. Her sword was in the air before Balor could even open the door.

His back tensed, and he cast a glance over his shoulder. "That is entirely unnecessary."

"That's fine," she said in a tight voice. "I think I'll keep it out just in case."

A hint of anger flickered through Balor's eye, along with resignation. If he still had the power of his Court, he could force a command onto Moira. She would have to put her sword away, if he insisted. While Balor had always respected the power of his Princely bond, he still used it, especially in situations like this, ones that involved missions and danger and the future of the supernatural world.

I kind of thought the bond sucked, if I were being honest. No one should be magically forced to do anything against their will, not even by their powerful Prince.

But I didn't make the rules, now did I?

When Nemain had taken control of the Court, that power had been stripped from Balor. He'd not only lost the unstoppable flames of his eye. He'd lost his connection with the fae he'd devoted his entire life to protecting.

"Wait here," he said. "When I give you the all-clear, follow me."

Moira and I exchanged a glance as Balor pushed inside the catacombs. We waited half a beat before traipsing in after him. Orders smorders. We weren't about to let him go into the depths of dangerous dungeons all by his lonesome.

He might be Balor Beimnech, but he wasn't indestructible.

Close, but not quite.

A growl of irritation eked through his parted lips just as the dank darkness filled with the eerie sound of scuttling. An icy finger slipped down my spine, dread pooling in my veins.

It was the sound of the Sluagh. They were here, and they were...

Well, they were *somewhere*. This place was cloaked in shadows, but a glimmer of light rippled across

Moira's fae sword, enough to highlight the crumbling center gallery and the many aisles that forked off to coffins unknown. Other than that, I could spot a lot of dirt and a lot of cobwebs. A few rats flashed their beady little eyes in our direction, and then scurried off.

"Um." Moira inched forward, her heavy boots scuffing the dust-covered floor. "Our Sluagh pals appear to be missing."

"Oh, they're not missing." I shivered. "I can hear them. And smell them."

The scent of death and decay swirled into my nostrils, and a chorus of hisses poured into my ears. I wet my lips, sliding my steel from the sheath belted around my waist.

Ahead of us, Balor's hand found his sword. He held his weapon before him. It should have made me feel better, but it did nothing to calm my fear. If he felt a blade was necessary, the Sluagh definitely weren't our friendly neighborhood mindless fae anymore.

Three cloaked figures scuttled out of the darkness. Their faces were obscured by shadows, but thin bony fingers poked out from their sleeves as they raised their own blood-caked weapons in the air.

"Erm." I tightened the grip on my sword. "So, it looks like they've started decaying."

Moira grimaced. "Also, they found a stash of maces. Did some bloody idiot store some maces in a coffin or something?"

"This isn't going according to plan," Balor said. "They've only been like this for a few weeks, at most. The disintegration process should take much longer than this."

"Does that mean they've been above ground?" Moira asked through clenched teeth.

Balor gave an almost indiscernible shake of his head. "Impossible."

But there wasn't any more time for us to debate the probability of fae Sluagh escaping from their makeshift cage. All three were coming straight toward us on bony feet that threw clouds of dust into the air.

"Stand your ground!" Balor shouted as the trio of Sluaghs slammed into him with screeching cries. They swarmed around him, hacking away with their bloody weapons. Balor was fast. He parried one blow and then the next, using his sword to defend his ground.

Moira shot one glance my way, her golden eyes full of fire. I nodded. She nodded. And then we ran.

But before we could reach our Prince, a heavy gust of black smoke slammed into us, knocking us twenty metres back. My knees knocked against the ground, pain slicing through me. Sucking in a deep breath, I slammed my knuckle into the ground and looked up. Balor had also fallen. The Sluagh surrounded him. He held up his sword to block their blows, but his movements had become sluggish. The air had been knocked from his lungs.

Fear tore through me like a hurricane. Tears stung my eyes. Balor was in trouble. My lover. My mate. My twin soul.

As tears slipped down my face, my fists clenched even tighter around the dirt. My lungs shuddered as I breathed, my body barely holding on from the tornado of emotions that were wracking every single cell inside of me.

I couldn't lose him. Not like this. Not ever.

JENNA WOLFHART

A Sluagh raised the mace higher in the air just as Balor turned his attention on another. The world slowed all around me as I saw exactly what would happen next. The mace would slam down on his head. Blood would pour from his skin. And that bright, brilliant light inside of him would drift away into the darkness.

A gurgled cry ripped from my throat as I slammed my fists against the ground, the force of my emotions hurtling from my open, screaming mouth. The force of my own voice sliced against my eardrums. I slammed my hands over my ears and winced, eyes wide as a strange black magic lifted the dirt from the floor and threw it straight at the Sluagh. The ground reverberated beneath me. The walls shook.

And then the Sluagh fell.

No one moved. No one spoke. Hell, I was pretty sure none of us even breathed for a good solid minute.

Slowly, Balor stood, glancing down at the Sluagh around his feet. When he lifted his eyes to mine, something flickered deep within him, and then it was gone.

"So, that's a new trick, huh?" Moira asked with a shaky laugh. "Still don't think you're somehow related to the Morrigan?"

"I have *nothing* to do with the Morrigan." My heart thumped.

"Normal fae cannot do things like this, Clark." Balor gestured around him. "You might not want to think you're connected to our immortalised Queen, but this right here proves you are."

7

*A*fter enduring more Morrigan chat, the three of us gathered up the unconscious Sluagh— one of whom was indeed Maeve—and moved them to a smaller, much more secure underground catacomb. Unfortunately (or fortunately, depending on how you looked at it), those three were it. The rest of the fae Sluagh had vanished.

Step one of our insane mission: complete. Next up, it was time to find that sorcerer.

~

*A*fter a very fitful night of sleep, the sorcerer requested to meet us at Cereal Killer Cafe. We all piled inside, sans Kyle, who was studiously listening to us through three identical, indeterminable microphones attached to our shirts. The walls were lined with colourful boxes of American cereal, most of which I'd thought was banned in England. Just looking at them gave me a sugar coma.

There was a line queuing out the door, while the tables inside were packed to the brim with customers slurping milk and sugar, chomping away happily.

A twenty-something guy with long blonde hair stood up in the far corner, waving us over. He wore a purple cloak and a hat to match, bright neon stars painted on haphazardly. He even held a golden staff in his hand.

I glanced at Moira. "I think maybe we've been scammed."

Moira snorted, her body shaking with silent laughter. "So, when he said sorcerer for hire what he really meant was the Mickey Mouse kind of sorcerer. Should we go say hi to Merlin or cut our losses and go back home?"

"I ordered some cereal for you!" the guy called out in a high-pitched, nasally voice. My stomach grumbled in response.

"Well, it would be rude not to stay," I said.

Balor rolled his eyes. "This is a waste of time."

"Hey," a girl at the cash register leaned out, poking her head through the line of customers. "We're super busy. Either go sit down with your friend or go outside. Please."

I looped my hand through Balor's arm and tried to bite back my smile. "Come on. We do need to eat, you know."

Balor grumbled, but he didn't pry himself away as we dragged him toward the back booth were the "sorcerer" waited for us. He'd slumped back down into his seat and leaned over a massive bowl of purple and pink marshmallows. He pointed at a cluster of bowls on the table, all filled with the same cereal, along with some bottles of milk. "Ordered for you. Help your-selves. Name's Jake, by the way."

"Nice to meet you, Jake." I pulled the bowl toward me, grabbed the milk. "I'm Clark. This is Moira, and…Bal—um, Ball. His name is Ball."

Mentally, I kicked myself. Humans were more than aware of the former Prince of the Crimson Court. They all knew his name. Not many knew what he looked like. I was hoping this fake sorcerer dude was the latter.

"Don't worry. I know who he is, and I won't cause a scene." He paused in his shovelling of food and pushed a bowl toward Balor. "I'm like a mercenary. I don't care who my boss is. All I care about is getting paid. You give me money? We're all good."

I pursed my lips. "Listen. About that. We appreciate you coming all the way here to meet us. And for the cereal, of course. But when we saw your ad, we thought you were *really* a sorcerer. Like, one who can do real magic."

He chomped his way through another mouthful of cereal, nodding. "It's the outfit, isn't it? See, I didn't know you were fae, or I wouldn't have worn this. I made the same mistake with some vamps. They wouldn't even sit and have the cereal. Humans really lap it up though."

Moira glanced at me, eyebrows raised. "Wait, so you're the real deal?"

"Yeah, like I said, humans. They're pretty skeptical unless you look the part." He gestured down at his robe, pointed at his staff. "So, I make sure to look the part when I'm meeting prospective clients. Of course, the humans rarely have actual supernatural problems.

I just indulge them. Why argue when a payday is involved, am I right?"

Huh. Well, okay then. This whole thing was weird, but...most sorcerers were pretty weird, I'd found. The last one I'd met had been seriously deranged and existed outside of reality.

"Most sorcerers don't like to be so conspicuous," Balor said quietly. "Especially in the current environment, here in London. They don't want to be lumped in with the supernaturals."

Jake took another big bite. "I'm not like most sorcerers. I like my magic, and I like to use it. Besides, a lad's gotta make a living somehow, right? Well, I'm not too good at most things, but I'll tell you what. I'm really, really good at magic."

I shot a glance at Balor, then at Moira. This situation hadn't gone at all like we'd expected, but we had found exactly what we'd come looking for. If this guy truly was a sorcerer, we might actually have a chance to undo the Sluagh spell on Maeve. And it didn't seem as though it would take much convincing to get him to do it.

"We're going to need some proof, " Balor finally said. "A demonstration that you are who you say you are."

Jake snorted. "A demonstration? Are you 'avin a laugh?"

Balor kept his gaze steady on the wannabe sorcerer. "Do I look like I'm having a laugh?"

"Nah, mate," Jake said. "Doubt you've ever had a laugh in your life."

He didn't know how close to the truth that really was.

"Alright," he said, after a moment's silence filled the space between us and him. "I'll put on a show for you if you insist. Hell, maybe it'll get me some more business if the humans here like what they see."

"No need to do anything flashy," I said, flicking my gaze at the long line of customers trailing out the open front door. "We're trying to keep a low profile."

"Don't worry," he said with a grin. "No one will know it was us."

He shot a glance over his shoulder, and his eyes sparked with delight. I had a bad feeling about this. Jake did not seem like the type who cared much for keeping his head down and operating beneath the radar. If his clothing was any indication, he liked being *loud*.

With his robes whispering around his ankles, he pushed up from the table and sashayed his way behind the counter. A bushy-haired girl barely gave him any notice. There was a slight pause when she turned to grab a box of Rice Krispies from the shelf behind her, but nothing more.

She muttered beneath her breath, but her words were still loud enough for me to hear. "Not again, Jake. I'm sick of your games."

His grin widened, and he turned to give our table a wink.

"I mean, he's going to have to do better than annoy someone," Moira muttered. "He seems to have a knack for it, but I'm pretty sure that's not magic."

"Wait," Balor said, a single brow winging upward. "I think there's more to this than meets the eye."

But I did not see what Balor could possibly mean. All the sorcerer was doing was standing beside the frazzled cereal barista with a creepy-ass smile pasted on his face.

After a long, strange moment passed, he whirled toward us and clapped his hands. And then he did the one thing I never would have expected. He braced his palms flat on the counter and then leapt up into the air.

His feet slammed on the wooden surface, and a loud smack echoed through the tiny cafe. I braced myself, gritting my teeth, fully expecting the humans to lose their ever-loving shit and flee.

But they didn't do a damn thing.

They continued to gaze nonchalantly at the cereal girl at the counter, instead of gazing up at the lunatic stomping around and waving his hands in the air.

"Magic clearly makes people go mad," Moira said. "Someone get him down from there before the humans charge at us."

"I don't think they're going to charge," I murmured, watching their expressions. Jake's dance had been going on for at least five minutes now, and a human had even paid for her cereal and sat down, all without the slightest bit of a reaction to his counter party. "As crazy as it sounds, I don't think they can see him."

Jake suddenly jumped off the counter and in front of the next human who was rattling off an order. He opened his mouth, leaned in close, and screamed right into her face.

No response. She didn't even flinch.

Jake whirled toward us, beaming.

"Okay, I think you've proven your point," Balor said dryly.

Jake wandered back over to us, giving the humans a shy little wave. When he was a meter away from our table, his form shimmered.

"That's quite the trick," I told him when he settled back into his seat.

"So, tell me the deal." Jake went back to chomping loudly through his cereal as if nothing at all had happened. "Why are three powerful fae here to hire a sorcerer?"

Balor cleared his throat and lowered his voice. "How much do you know about Sluagh?"

Jake's chewing slowed to a stop. "I know they're not to be fucked with. Please tell me that is not what this is about."

"I'm afraid so," I said with a frown. "So, they're not really in your wheelhouse then."

"Look." He set down his spoon. "A few months ago, I met a chap whose wheelhouse definitely *was* the Sluagh. The whole thing drove him absolutely mad. Last I heard, he went missing. The Sluagh probably killed him and ate him for tea. I have no desire to have the same fate."

Balor and I exchanged a glance. Obviously, he was talking about Eoin, a sorcerer that definitely had been killed but not by the Sluagh. My raven friends had taken care of him instead. Probably best not to tell this guy that though.

"The Sluagh can be dangerous," Balor said carefully. "Which is why I'm sure you agree that London would be better off if none were on its streets."

Jake lifted his brows to the top of his head. "And I suppose you have a way to do that? And it involves me?"

JENNA WOLFHART

"There's a spell," I said. "One that can totally undo the Sluagh curse. We need you to find it and cast it. It'll transform all the Sluagh back to their normal selves. Everyone wins."

"Everyone except for me. When they eat me."

"They won't eat you," Moira said with a roll of her eyes. "That's not what they do."

"Well, it's kind of what they do," I muttered.

"I don't care what they do." He crossed his arms over his chest. "I'm not getting even a pinky toe anywhere near them."

I exchanged another glance with Balor. This was clearly not going as well as we'd hoped. Not that I could blame this weird sorcerer. I'd fought the Sluagh on numerous occasions and every single time it had sucked royal arse. They were scary as hell, and they could do a lot of damage when they wanted to.

"We'll be there protecting you," I said. "We won't let them get anywhere near you. All we need is for you to cast the spell."

"And you have it? This spell of yours?"

"Erm. No. We hoped you'd be able to find it."

"Me? Find it?" He dropped back his head and laughed so hard that a hush fell heavily on Cereal Killer Cafe. "If you really expect me to go on the hunt for a spell and then go up against Sluagh, you're going to have to do something for me. And you're sure as hell not going to like it."

8

Narrowing my eyes, I slammed my hands on the table and leaned forward, hissing my words. "Keep your voice down."

He gave a nonchalant wave. "I'm mates with the owners of this fine establishment. They don't mind magic. Or fae. If you didn't notice, they don't have one of those ridiculous signs up."

By *ridiculous signs*, Jake meant the increasingly common notice that fae, vampires, and werewolves were not welcome in certain establishments, mainly human stores and restaurants. A few weeks ago, those signs had been practically nonexistent. Now, over half the shops in London had one.

"Those signs do not concern me," Balor said. "Tell me your payment terms."

Balor, getting right down to business, as per usual.

Even though Nemain had seized control of the Court, she had not successfully taken over Balor's bulging bank account. He had spent his entire life building a massive empire of wealth, of which he

JENNA WOLFHART

mostly used to look after the fae of London. He was a billionaire at this point. Nemain, on the other hand, wasn't.

Which was to say, he could pay this sorcerer any price he demanded.

Jake shrugged. "I don't want your money. I want your connections. I want a meeting with the Circle of Night."

Two thin lines appeared between Balor's eyebrows. "Matteo and I are not currently on good terms. He did not answer the call when the safety of this city depended on it."

Jake leaned back in his chair and laced his hands behind his head. "From where I'm sitting, the safety of this city has improved since Nemain took control. So, that would be a false statement."

Balor growled.

"See. You have a bit of a temper." The sorcerer shifted toward me. "Either way, I need this meeting. Can you get it for me?"

I nibbled my bottom lip. Matteo had strangely approached me after Balor had kicked me out of the Court—temporarily. He'd been chatty and had made it a point to let me know that he'd taken my side in the end. At first, I thought he'd been up to some kind of sinister plan, but that had been the end of it. Would he be willing to speak to this sorcerer if I asked?

"I guess it wouldn't hurt to try," I finally said.

"Clark," Balor said sharply. "He didn't heed the call of our alliance. Because of him, we no longer have control of the throne."

"I know. But we kind of need this. If it means returning the Sluagh back to their true forms..."

INNOCENT UNTIL PROVEN FAE

Balor frowned, but he didn't argue. Instead, he ground his teeth together and gave me a nod. "Fine. But you take the lead on this. If I have to see Matteo right now, I might end up punching him in the face."

$\approx$

*M*oira and I strode inside the Circle of Night while Jake waited outside with Balor. No one stopped us, which suggested that they'd spotted us far before we'd opened the front door. I took a deep breath and looked around. The old Lutine Bell stood solemnly in the center of the floor with the great Loss Book squatting beside it. The vampires had seized this building from the humans when they'd decided they wanted a financial control center in the heart of London. From here, the Circle of Night did…who knew what, to be honest. I knew it was heavy on the finance side, light on the ethics.

Awhile back, some of their members had gotten involved in an illegal trade of shifter blood. They had been capturing and killing wolves of the Pack, in order to harvest their blood. Blood that was deadly to…well, other vampires.

A pretty shitty operation if you asked me.

At the time, Matteo had been livid because the black market blood trade group had taken his own son as prisoner, since he had shifter blood running through his veins. But I'd always wondered…if the group hadn't targeted his family, would he have put a stop to the operation?

I wasn't so sure.

But before I could reach the Loss Book, a familiar

figure decked in all white stepped in front of me. The vampire's teeth flashed beneath the luminous glittering lights that filled up the building, the bleached colour matching his salt white hair.

"Clark Cavanaugh," he said in a smooth, baritone voice. "I must admit, I am shocked to find you paying a visit to the Circle of Night." His eyes flicked to the door behind me. "Particularly with a certain fae Prince who is no longer a Prince at all."

"Don't worry. He's not coming inside."

He arched a perfectly-manicured brow. "Why on earth would I be worried?"

"You kind of backed out of your promised alliance," I said flatly. "You know, when Nemain took over his Court?"

"I made the only decision I could. You would have done the same."

"Highly unlikely."

He pursed his lips, flicking his eyes up and down my short frame. "One day you will remember."

I blinked at him. "Huh? Remember what?"

Moira cleared her throat, carefully steering me back to the entire reason we'd come here in the first place.

"Right." I frowned. "Is there somewhere we can talk?"

"Here is fine."

I arched a brow. "You don't trust us in your office?"

He nodded toward the front door of the building. "*You* are fine. I wish to keep an eye on Balor. I know his feelings toward me have…soured."

"Fine. We can talk here. You clearly knew we were

INNOCENT UNTIL PROVEN FAE

coming. So, you must also know that we brought a sorcerer along with us," I said, getting straight to the point.

"Yes," he mused. "I did wonder at that. Surely you don't intend to try and cast a spell on my Circle as some sort of silly revenge plot?"

"Of course not. Don't be so dramatic."

He pursed his lips. "Alright then. Do tell."

"Right. Here's the deal. We've asked the sorcerer to do us a favour. A magical kind of favour. In return, he asked for me to get him a meeting with you."

"Asked *you*?" He chuckled. "How extraordinarily interesting."

"It really isn't that interesting," I said flatly, turning to Moira. "I think he just assumed that I would have a better chance speaking to you than Balor would."

Moira nodded. "That sorcerer is pretty damn weird, but he isn't a muppet."

"A sorcerer who keeps up with supernatural politics," Matteo mused, rustling his white hair as he spoke. "Do you not find that curious?"

"No more curious than your decision to back out of the alliance when the fight came to London."

"Not curious at all, love," Matteo said. "I chose what was best for my family."

"I'm sure that's what you think."

"And what does this sorcerer friend of yours want?"

I shrugged. "That's not important."

"Oh, I disagree," he said, the tone of his voice turning icy. "I do not trust a magic-wielder who does not make his intentions known."

"I didn't take you for the type to fear a sorcerer."

JENNA WOLFHART

"Careful," he murmured, eyes glittering. "I like you, Clark, but I do not like you that much."

I decided to call his bluff. "Actually, I think you like me more than you like to let on."

He let out a low chuckle. "Tell you what. You share with me why you're so desperate for me to meet with this sorcerer, and I'll agree to do it."

My nostrils flared as I took in the leader of the Circle of Night. Calm, perfectly-put-together, but there was a tension in the tips of his fingers. Every so often, they twitched. He wanted to know the truth. Badly.

Could I trust him? He hadn't fought on our side, but he hadn't fought against us either. And we desperately needed the sorcerer's help. Without it, we had no hope of undoing the Sluagh spell.

"Swear it," I said. "Swear it on the Lutine Bell."

He pursed his lips, the corners tilting up. "Clever. All right. I swear it."

I puffed out a breath. "Good." And then I filled him in on our plan. When I'd finished the story, he looked far less impressed than he had two seconds ago.

"Why was I not made aware of this Sluagh situation until now?" His voice was icy and hard as steel. "As the leader of the most prestigious vampiric society in London, I should be told when there are dangerous developments that can affect the entire supernatural world."

"We just thought it was best to keep the information as contained as possible, along with the Sluagh. The fewer people who know, the better."

"*We?*" His brows shot up. "Or *Balor*? I find it difficult to believe you were involved in this unfortunate decision."

I wet my lips. I couldn't really blame him for being angry, but I wasn't about to place all the blame on my Prince, even if it *had* been his decision. "Balor listens to his advisors."

He snorted. "You're loyal, too. Can't say I'm surprised. Just remember that loyalty is often a two-edged sword. You think you're swinging the blade at your enemy, but you can just as easily get cut yourself."

I let out a frustrated sigh. "Look, I'm sorry we didn't tell you until now, but there's nothing I can do at this point to change it. And now you can see why we need this sorcerer's help. If you meet with him, he'll take care of the problem. That's what you want, isn't it?"

He shot me a smile full of glittering teeth. "Oh yes. I want that very much. In fact, it's important enough that we need to ensure the sorcerer is *properly* motivated. Just to be certain of his intentions."

Well, shit. I really didn't like the sound of this.

"He's not a fan of Sluagh either," I said flatly. "Pretty sure he's properly motivated to take care of the situation."

Matteo took a step closer, bringing with him a whiff of whiskey and iron. "You might be surprised at just how self-serving these sorcerers can be. Tell him that I will meet with him, and that I will give him exactly what he wants—immortality. But I will only do so after he's rid London of these Sluagh."

I opened my mouth to argue, but Matteo held up a hand to stop me. "Don't bother denying it. He may not have told you what he wants from me, but I have no doubt that immortality is it. He will ask if he can become one of us."

Shaking my head, I took a step back to put space between the two of us. "You don't do that anymore. The Circle hasn't changed a human in years."

"The times have changed. Peace has left us."

"Balor won't like it."

"Balor," Matteo said with a glittering smile, "is not in charge anymore. Go ask the sorcerer himself. He will tell you that is what he wants. And I will give it to him, after he undoes the curse."

9

*O*utside, Balor and Jake were waiting for us. I stared hard at the sorcerer, plunging my mind into his head. His thoughts flittered around like wispy things. Sorcerers were not supernatural beings, like vampires, fae, and werewolves were. They were humans, endowed with ability to use magic. That made his mind far easier to read than fae.

Hope she's been able to get me that meeting. Eternal life, here I come.

I scowled and pulled myself out of his brain, poking a finger right into his chest. He blinked and stumbled back. "You haven't been totally honest with us."

"You can say that again," Moira mumbled beneath her breath.

"What are you talking about?" He glanced from me to Moira and back again. "Of course I have."

"You happened to leave out the part where you want to become a vampire."

His face blanched. "I didn't think it was important."

I snorted and turned toward Balor. "That's why he wanted a meeting with Matteo. Unfortunately, Matteo isn't an idiot, and he figured it out quicker than we did. So, he knows he has leverage. He refuses to do a damn thing until this muppet," I said, jerking a thumb toward the sorcerer, "does what we've asked."

Balor's expression darkened. "I cannot support this. It was a long, hard road to get the vampires to stop attacking humans. I do not wish for them to get a taste for it again."

"Ain't your decision, mate," Jake replied with a shrug. "If Matteo agrees to turn me, then I don't see how it's any of your business what I willingly want to do to my body."

"Can I talk to Balor alone for a minute?" I asked Jake. I flicked my eyes toward Moira, who gave a nod.

"I'll treat you to some fish and chips. There's a good place right around the corner." She took Jake's elbow in her hand and steered him away from us.

After they'd disappeared around the corner, Balor kept his gaze on the horizon, staring after them. "I don't want things to return to how they once were. I was worried this would happen when Nemain took control. I just didn't expect it to happen so quickly." He turned to me with a glittering eye. "Matteo agreed to turn him, yes?"

I blew out a hot breath. "He said he'd do it if Jake got rid of the Sluagh, who he seemed to be legitimately worried about. Like you, I think Matteo is just trying to do the right thing for London."

"So, you agree that we should allow the vampires

to go back to turning humans. It's a dangerous ritual, Clark." He turned to face me, took my hands in his. "Fewer than half of humans can survive it. Back then, the vamps didn't care. It took a lot of convincing for me to get Matteo to stop."

I hadn't known that Balor was the one directly responsible for putting an end to the changing ritual, but I wasn't surprised. He'd done so much to try and change the world, to make it a better place, and he'd succeeded. Now, all of it, everything he'd worked for, was sitting on top of a precipice, ready to fall.

"Balor," I whispered, reaching up so that my palm rested on his face. A shockwave of desire shot through my gut, just from the smallest of touches. Fire sparked in his orange-red eye, reflecting the heat of my core.

Suddenly, I no longer recalled what we'd been discussing. All I could think about was his hands on my skin, his lips brushing against my thighs. It took all my self-control not to moan out loud, right there in the middle of the street outside of the Circle of Night.

"What's happening?" I whispered.

"We're mated," he said in a voice that rumbled from deep within his throat. "And we've only *just* mated."

"That doesn't explain why it feels like every part of me is on fire." And I did mean *every* part.

"Oh yes, it certainly does." He wrapped his hand behind my head and slipped his fingers through my hair, curling them tight around the strands. The whole thing practically left me as a humming puddle on the floor. "When fae first mate, their desire for each other is practically endless. All it takes is a single touch for…well, *this*."

This was beyond anything I'd felt before. My body practically pulsed, my skin tingling with a magical force that hurtled through my very soul. All I could think about was Balor. How desperate I was to be as close to him as I could possibly be. How heat emanated from his muscular body. How he drank me in with his flaming eye.

I shuddered and leaned into his touch. A part of me, the logical part that remembered exactly where we were, tried to pull away from him. But that part was far too weak to fight against the magic of our mating bond.

It was so intense that it almost scared me.

But only almost.

"We should probably go," I whispered, not meaning my words even a little. "Moira and Jake are waiting for us."

"Weren't you going to try and convince me to let Matteo change the human?"

Oh yeah. "Are you convinced?"

He shook his head, and then smiled. "No, but I can think of a few things that might work to convince me."

My heart thumped hard. "We are outside in the City of London, on the pavement by the front door of the Circle of Night. Matteo is likely watching."

"Let him watch," he growled, but then he lifted me off the ground and strode toward the alley between the vampire building and the next.

Shadows fell across us as Balor ducked between the two towering walls that would protect us from gazes of innocent passersby. He slammed me up against the bricks, knocking the breath from my lungs.

Magic pulsed beneath my skin, swarming up to my lips as his mouth found mine.

I moaned and squeezed my thighs tightly around his hips, grinding my body against his. His length was already hard. He was pressed so tightly against me that I could feel the entire outline of him burning against me. His power pulsed into me, combining with my own magic in a twisting, tumbling tornado. My hair flew around my shoulders, whipping against his face and mine.

He pulled back, panting, and stared deeply into my eyes.

It was then I noticed the entire alley had been transformed. A deep, unsettling darkness had descended around us, shot through with sparks of electricity that zigged and zagged from one wall to the next. Magic swirled over our heads, in the form of bursting clouds that sprayed shards of ice in the air.

I sucked in a breath and stared at the raw power displayed here.

"Is that…normal?" I asked in a small voice. I'd known that mating was powered by some serious magic, but this was something else entirely. It was like it had come from the very depths of Faerie itself, from a different world hidden deep beneath our feet.

Balor's voice was awed when he spoke. "I have never mated with anyone before, but I have heard tales of it. This is nothing like the legends."

My heart thumped. "Do you think it's dangerous?"

He dropped his gaze from the darkness to my eyes. "I think it speaks to the power of our bond."

A ripple of carnal desire went through me. I wrapped my arms tight around his neck, letting myself give in to the heat pulsing between our bodies. His dark, powerful magic wrapped around me as he reached down and unzipped my jeans.

His length pulsed between my legs as he entered me. Dropping back my head, I moaned, hair cascading all around my shoulders. The unsettling darkness swirled around us like black flames, sparks lighting up my skin in time with his thrusts.

He wrapped his hands around my wrists and pinned them to the wall. His mouth dropped to my neck, hot lips stealing across my skin. I writhed against him, squeezing my thighs tight around his hips. The logical part of my brain noticed a few passersby casting furtive glances our way, but my body wouldn't listen.

"You're my mate," Balor growled as his teeth nicked my skin. My neck flamed from where he'd left a mark.

Sliding my hand up his back, I dug in my nails. I needed the world to know he was mine. I scratched down the length of him, and he growled out his approval.

It was all I could do not to scream his name so loud that it would echo all the way to Heathrow.

He continued to pulse against me, slamming my body hard against the wall. I clung on tight, crying out as my entire soul was consumed by him. The power built and built until every single part of us was hidden in the smoke. The darkness slammed hard against the wall, and chunks of brick fell to the ground.

"Balor," I whispered, momentarily forgetting our passion for the storm brewing around us. The wind had gotten out of control now. It was kicking up rubbish with frantic energy, throwing my hair into my face.

He grasped my chin in his hand and forced my gaze back on to him. "Don't worry about that right now. Just focus on me."

And so the storm consumed us.

10

*M*oira arched a brow when we ambled through the front door of the fish and chips shop. "So, you two have mated then, huh? That explains some things."

My cheeks flamed. Balor cleared his throat. The sorcerer looked amused.

"That's actually a real thing?" Jake laughed. "Brilliant. That mean you two get the magical dangly bits and have to shag all the time?"

The flames went from my cheeks through the rest of my skull.

A low growl rumbled from Balor's throat. Jake's face blanched.

Moira patted the sorcerer's shoulder. "Probably best not to talk about his mate's dangly bits, magical or otherwise."

"Noted." He cleared his throat. "So, we, uh, all good? With the whole vampy business?"

I winced and glanced up at Balor. We hadn't actu-

JENNA WOLFHART

ally…discussed the whole vampy thing. Well, we'd started to, but we'd never finished the conversation.

Balor frowned, those twin lines appearing between his eyebrows. "I am not sure you understand the risks involved."

We eased into the booth, and the faux leather crinkled beneath my legs. A few humans glanced over at us, frowned. Moira and Jake had ordered a big serving of chips, and the sight of it made my stomach rumble. I lifted my hand and waved over the server, but she bustled toward another table instead.

Jake rolled his eyes and took a big slurp of his drink. I was starting to think this sorcerer had an unending appetite. He hadn't stopped eating since we'd met him in the cafe. "I understand the consequences just fine, thanks. The vamp changes me, and I become one of them. Immortal life, money, status. Seems like a pretty sweet deal if you ask me."

This lad only had it half-right. But life in vampire land wasn't quite as easy as it looked.

"You may end up with your 'pretty sweet deal' as you call it, *if* you survive the change." Balor placed his palms flat on the table and leaned forward. "You have apparently been researching the vamps. Did your human study books tell you what the chances of you surviving are? Because you might be surprised to find out."

"Balor," I said in warning. Scaring the shit out of the sorcerer probably wasn't the most ideal way to get him to do what we needed him to do.

"He should understand what he's asking for." Balor pushed off the table, leaned back into the crinkly booth. "Otherwise, we will just have to find

INNOCENT UNTIL PROVEN FAE

another sorcerer who is willing to help us. One without a death sentence hanging over his head."

"No, no." The sorcerer held up his hands. "I'll listen to what you have to say. So, go on then. What are the odds?"

"Fewer than half of humans can survive it, which means your chances of living through the change is less than fifty percent. I would estimate it is more like forty."

The sorcerer pursed his lips, and then went back to slurping his drink. "It is worth it. If I survive the change, then I will be one of the most powerful sorcerers in the world."

Ah, so that was it. Just like everyone else, Jake wanted power.

"Isn't magic enough?" I asked, arching a brow. "Hell, you can make yourself invisible. Why do you need to become a vampire as well?"

"Immortality." His eyes flickered. "My first choice? I would become a fae if I could, but there is no way for a human to transform into that. A vampire will do."

Balor drummed his fingers on the table. I didn't need to read his mind to know that he wasn't a fan of Jake's motives. Those who seek power for the sake of power usually do not deserve it. And if we agreed to this, Balor would have to keep his word.

"Fine," Balor finally said in a dangerous voice. "But this is for you and you alone. None of your sorcerer friends can join in on this. Do you understand? I will agree to one person, but we cannot let this become an epidemic."

Jake grinned. "Why would I want to share my

power with anyone else? If every sorcerer in the city turned vamp, I wouldn't be special, now would I?"

I fought the urge to roll my eyes.

"Good." Balor braced his hands on the table and leaned back into his seat. "Then, it is a deal."

Out of the corner of my eye, something flashed. I turned to spot a human lurking behind an artificial plant whose drooping leaves had seen many better days. He was a small squat man with pizza stains all over his white t-shirt, but his camera looked as though it cost a million bucks. He snapped another picture, the flash filling the entire restaurant with bright white light.

Balor frowned in his direction, and the photographer scuttled away down a short hallway signposted with toilet signs. It was then that I noticed every single human in the place was staring at our table. Several were whispering. Others held up their phones, as if recording the scene.

The server finally flittered by our table, winced, and then pointed at a framed sign on the wall on the opposite end of the restaurant. My stomach churned. The sign was clear enough. It read:

NO FAE ALLOWED.

"Er, Balor," I said, pulling on his sleeve. "Looks like we're not welcome here."

"Oh yeah." The sorcerer popped a chip into his mouth. "Forgot about that. They just put that sign up last week."

"Might have been good to mention that earlier," I said through gritted teeth.

Balor frowned. "I really do not want to be seen as

a fae who goes running every time a damn sign tells him he's not welcome. We'll stay."

"Bad idea, mate." The sorcerer threw a few bills on the table and stood quickly from his chair. "The humans have formed a task force. Any minute now they'll show up, and they'll *make* you leave."

A low growl emanated from Balor's throat. "You do realise that we are stronger and faster. It wouldn't be a fair fight. Not for them."

The sorcerer shrugged. "That might be true, but there'll be a lot of them. Plus, I thought you didn't want to get any human blood on your hands."

Balor cursed beneath his breath.

"I don't like to run. It shows weakness." Still, he pushed up from the booth and motioned for Moira and me to follow. The entire restaurant fell silent as we got to our feet. The servers even paused in their tracks, plates balanced precariously on trembling hands.

They didn't want any trouble. We didn't want any trouble.

But everyone else? Fire stormed in their eyes.

"Listen," I said, holding up my hands and stepping into the middle of the aisle between tables. "We wish no harm on anyone here, or any other human in this city. We're leaving. Okay?"

No response. Everyone just continued to stare at me with expressions of pure, unbridled hatred.

"Right." I cleared my throat. "Well, this isn't awkward at all."

Slowly, I inched down the aisle of tables, heavy boots thumping against the sticky linoleum floor. When I reached the exit door, I released an inaudible sigh and pushed out into the London streets...only to

JENNA WOLFHART

find two dozen humans clustered around the restaurant...carrying cricket bats.

"Erm," I said.

"Let me handle this, Clark." Balor pushed past to stand at the front of our little team. Me, Moira, and a sorcerer who looked far too amused for my liking. I had a feeling this guy had been punched in the face more than a couple of times. And he'd deserved it.

"Faeries aren't welcome here." A tall, bulky man stepped forward, smacking his bat against his open palm. He wore a tight black tank that did little to hide a pretty impressive set of biceps. His skin had been tanned to a shade eerily close to orange, and when he flashed his teeth, the brilliant white of them almost blinded me.

Moira muttered beneath her breath.

"What's that?" I asked, arching a brow, but keeping my gaze firmly on the human mob.

"Reality star," she said, whispering a little louder. "Couple Island this last season. I liked him until he mugged off Serena for a new bombshell."

I cut my eyes her way.

"What?" She shrugged. "Everyone deserves a guilty pleasure."

"Enough." Mr. Reality Star glared in our direction. "You've come onto a property where you are no longer allowed. There will be repercussions for your actions."

Balor growled.

"Maybe let's not growl at the angry humans," I tried to hiss to him through our mental bond. But, if he heard my thoughts, he didn't heed them.

"You have no authority over us." Balor stood taller,

INNOCENT UNTIL PROVEN FAE

power rippling off his skin in vicious waves. "We were leaving. If you insist on taking this issue to fight, then I am afraid you will come to regret it. Deeply."

I fought the urge to roll my eyes. Balor was incredibly talented at a good many things, but with angry human negotiation? Not so much.

The sorcerer cleared his throat and gave a little wave to Balor, his star-studded cloak billowing in the thick city air. "Hi."

Balor stiffened and glanced back at Jake. "Not now."

"Well, as it happens, I know Pete Pritchard here. I did a job for him awhile back." Another throat clear.

Translation: he'd scammed the dude. Hopefully, the reality star hadn't realised.

Pete Pritchard narrowed his eyes, bushy brows coming together to form a caterpillar. "That you, Jake?"

"The one and only."

"What are you doing with these faeries? They're bad news, mate."

"Nah, these fae aren't so bad." Jake shrugged and stepped forward. "They want no trouble. As soon as they saw the sign, they decided to leave. Good enough, eh?"

Pete frowned, but then he took a step back and shrugged. "Yeah, guess that's good enough. We don't want to stoop to their level, eh?"

"Exactly." Jake grinned and then motioned for us to follow him down the pavement. "See you around, Pete. Oh, and congrats on reaching two mil followers on Insta. You're killing it."

"Thanks, mate. And careful with those faeries.

They might seem well nice now, but they're not to be trusted."

Balor was stiff and silent as we strode away from the angry humans. He was...not happy, to say the least. Truth was, I wasn't either. If Jake hadn't been with us, there was no telling what would have happened. We desperately needed to soothe the relationship between the supe and non-supe populations, but how would we do that unless we ended this war with Nemain?

Just another reason why we needed to get the cure ASAP.

As we strode down the London streets, I dropped back and blurred into the crowd. It wouldn't take long for Balor to notice that I'd vanished from his side, so I had to make this quick. I dug out my cell and dialled a familiar number.

A moment later, the line clicked. "If you needed to talk to me, you could have just spoken into the microphone."

"Hey Kyle," I said, whispering into the phone. "I need you to look something up for me."

"Is this Balor-approved?"

A beat passed. "What do you think?"

He sighed. "Why did I even ask? Of course it isn't. Nothing you ever do is Balor-approved."

"But, you're going to do it, right?" I asked.

"I really shouldn't," he mumbled. "But what is it?"

"I need you to look up something about a dark power. The kind that makes clouds and electricity." With a deep breath, I filled him in on the rest, careful not to mention where exactly the power had come from: our mating.

Kyle agreed to use his master searching skills, and then hung up the phone. I waited a moment before picking up my pace, catching my breath. There was something off with what had happened in the alley. Balor had admitted it wasn't normal. I didn't want it to freak me out, but I couldn't ignore the fact that it did. What if there was something wrong with our mating bond? What if the two of us together was the very thing that would put an end to this world?

It was too horrible an idea to even think it.

But I had to find out.

11

The underground haven for sorcerers pumped dubstep through twin loud speakers perched in the furthest corners of the cave. Smoke filled the air, along with a thick mist that smelled of berries. The crowd in the center of the rocky floor writhed and whirled and danced. Everyone was having the time of their lives, aided by some illegal substances, if their half-lidded, red-streaked eyes were any indication.

Jake leaned closer to shout into my ear. "Not everyone here is a sorcerer!"

"No shit, Sherlock," I muttered with a roll of my eyes. There were probably four hundred party-goers packed into this tiny cave, and human magic-wielders were much more uncommon than that. If I were to guess, London probably had around ten sorcerers. Tops.

"Once we get a taste of magic," he continued, "we get hooked on the rush of it, the adrenaline. So we start to crave other things." He waved at the corner where a couple of girls were handing out tiny ziplock bags of white pills. "It's the only way to feel what the magic makes us feel."

I arched my brows. "Why not just use your magic?"

"There are limits," he said with a shrug. "It's different for everyone, but we run hard into a wall eventually. It's like we have a limited supply of it. The only way to fill it back up again is to wait."

"So, in the meantime, you get your kicks other ways."

"Exactly." He flashed me a smile, and then waggled his eyebrows. "You get me. Maybe a sorcerer and a fae can get along better than people think. If you know what I mean."

Balor's hand fell heavily on his shoulder. "Careful. Just because she understands your inane blathering doesn't mean she agrees. And it most certainly doesn't mean she wants to jump into bed with you. She's my mate. Mine."

A flush of red crept up the sorcerer's neck. "Yeah, of course. I was just messing around. I didn't mean anything by it. Honestly."

"Balor." I placed a hand on his arm. "You need to calm down."

He let out a low growl in response. I frowned, but secretly, deep down inside, I felt a flush of satisfaction from his jealousy. Where we touched sparked with magic, and the bond between us snapped tight. I found myself in his arms, even though I didn't remember him reaching for me or me for him. I pressed myself up against him as hard as I could, desire pumping through my veins.

Moira rolled her eyes, and pulled the two of us

INNOCENT UNTIL PROVEN FAE

apart. "Get ahold of yourselves. Now is not the time. Save it for the flat. And please, for the love of the Morrigan, wait until I'm not around."

Chagrined, I pushed down the front of my shirt and tried to look at anyone and anything but Balor. Moira was right. This was kind of getting out of control. We needed to get a grip. There was far too much at stake for us to get distracted by our insatiable lust in the middle of a mission.

We pushed through the crowd, following the sorcerer. He led us to a dimly-lit back corner of the cave where a platform had been built. Stone steps led up to the dais-like space where long wooden benches full of people were clustered around a table full of booze and empty bags. In between us and them was a red rope, and a handwritten sign that said VIP.

Jake waved over a girl who wore a long, crimson cloak around broad shoulders. Her hair was just as red, trailing down her back where it hit her waist. She had about a dozen piercings on her face, and ten studs along her ears. When she stood from the group, they all fell silent.

"Elena," Jake said, grinning up at her. "Mind if me and my friends join you?"

She cast a bored look over our group. "Fae. Really, Jake? That's who you're hanging with these days? You really have lost your edge."

"Just you wait," he said with a grin. "In a week's time, your tune will change."

Suddenly, I understood what Jake was up to here. He had the hots for this sorcerer, who clearly did not have the same hots for him. For some crazy reason, he

JENNA WOLFHART

thought if he became a vampire, then she'd finally pay some attention to him.

I had a sneaking suspicion it wouldn't do him a lick of good.

Elena lifted a penciled eyebrow. "You say that every single week. I don't know why you think this one will be any different."

Interesting. So, this wasn't the first time Jake had tried to find a vampire willing to change him into one of them. I wondered what else he'd done, who else he'd tried to negotiate with. And I couldn't help but wonder just how far Jake was willing to go.

"It's different this time," he replied.

"I'm busy. Don't waste my time," she said in a bored voice. "What do you want?"

Jake waggled his eyebrows as he plonked next to the sorcerer. "I need a little peek inside your store of spell books."

"The store is only for coven members. You aren't a coven member."

I arched a brow. "Coven?"

Jake gave a vigorous nod. "London has its first coven. It's only been around a few months."

The sorcerer frowned. "What Jake doesn't seem to understand is that we'd rather keep its existence on the down low. Don't tell your fae friends."

I had a lot of questions. One, did she understand that covens and sorcery didn't really go together? They were a Wiccan thing, and as far as I could tell, sorcerers were not Wiccan. Two, why had they formed it? Third, and most importantly, why was she so insistent it be kept a secret?

The only logical answer? They were doing something they didn't want anyone else to know about, which likely meant it probably wasn't good.

These were all questions that needed to be answered, but I had a feeling if I questioned her, she'd refuse to hand over that spell book. Luckily, I didn't need to ask her out loud. The perk of being a fae with mind reading powers.

Taking a deep breath, I focused my mind on the sorcerer before me. I kept my eyes open, hoping they wouldn't glaze over as I prodded at her brain. Anyone who had ever seen me read a mind before would recognise the look on my face, but I'd only just met this girl.

I threw myself forward and pushed against the edges of her brain. A strange shock went through me, sparking a million tiny needles of pain up and down my arms. It threw me out of her head and right back into my own brain. When I jolted back to reality, her glittering eyes met mine.

"I think you'll find that I am not as unarmed as most humans are." She leaned forward and blew a smokey breath across my face. "Try it again, and you'll face far worse pain than that. Go on. Try me, fae."

"Nice one," I said in as nonchalant a voice as possible. Inwardly, my mind was reeling as Balor braced his hand against my back, but I couldn't let her see just how much her magic had shaken me. "How long did it take you to master that kind of spell?"

She smiled. "Much longer than you think."

I arched my brows. She couldn't be much older than twenty or twenty-one. As far as I knew, sorcerers didn't really come into their power until they'd passed puberty. Often, it took much longer than that.

"I know what you're thinking," she said, brushing her long red hair over her bony shoulders. "I look young, right? Sometimes, all is not what it seems."

I wasn't entirely sure what she meant by that. Truth be told, I probably didn't want to know. If she was delving into the darkest parts of magic, she was likely involved in far worse things than party drug distribution in this underground club.

"So, can we have the book?" Jake cut in, edging in front of me.

"You brought mind-reading fae into my territory. I really shouldn't be handing over this spell book to you." She waved her hand in dismissal. "Goodbye, Jake. I am done with this little game."

"She's going to introduce me to the vampire," he said quickly.

Elena froze mid-wave and an unsettling expression of intrigue flickered across her face. "Is that right?"

I frowned. "As long as he agrees to help us with one little thing, then yes, but—"

"Ooh." She clapped her hands, and her entire face transformed. No longer did she look at Jake with bored scorn, but a new spark of flirtation lit up in her eyes. She sidled a little closer to him, rubbing her side up against his arm. Jake's face went bright red. "I didn't think you had it in you. Maybe I've misjudged you all this time, Jakey."

I wrinkled my nose. *Jakey?* Really?

Balor scowled and dropped a heavy hand on Jake's shoulder, hauling him away from Elena. He yanked him through the crowd, effortlessly, stopping only when he came to a dark corner at the very back of the bar. "We had an agreement. No one else. Just you."

Jakey winced. "I wasn't trying to get her to join me in the vamp thing. I just know it's something she's wanted a long-ass time, and…well you saw her. She's hot."

My eyes rolled out of my head. "She's also a complete sociopath who will just use you to get what she wants."

"She can use me all she wants."

"No." Balor tightened his grip. "Go make this right, or we'll end this right here and now."

Jake swallowed hard and opened his mouth to argue. I shook my head before he could speak another word. "I wouldn't make his mood any worse than it already is, if I were you."

With a slow nod, Jake sighed. "Fine. But I'm only doing this for the deal you got me. Not because you're bullying me."

I rolled my eyes as Jake turned and scurried back through the crowd. He stopped at the edge of the VIP section, waving his hands emphatically at Elena. She pursed her lips and laughed. She was clearly as annoyed with Jake as we were.

But, a moment later, she stepped over the red velvet rope and disappeared into a hidden cave opening I hadn't spotted in the dark lighting of the club.

After several long moments, Jake came back with his metaphorical tail between his legs and clutching the spell book with white-knuckled fists. Balor reached out, but the sorcerer held it back, shaking his head.

"No fae. Only sorcerers." He tapped the top of the leather-bound book. "Elena only agreed to loan this to me on the basis that you won't touch it, not even with the tip of your pinky finger."

"Fine." Balor pressed his lips together into a thin, white line. "Have you confirmed the spell is in there?"

Jake nodded. "This is definitely the one."

"Good." Balor nodded. "And you're certain that you can perform it?"

"I've got a date with a vampire master if this works. So, yes. I'm certain."

"You better be."

12

When we made it to the street with the book firmly in hand, we found that we weren't the only visitors to Infinity that night. Several human policemen stood blocking our path, frowning down at the long passageway that led to the sorcerers' haven. Their cars hulked behind them. Blue lights flashed against the brick buildings. Overhead, several curious residents had opened their windows, heads poked out to watch the scene unfold.

A female cop with dark hair pulled back into a tight ponytail stepped forward when we pushed out into the night. "We got a report that you were here. Didn't think you'd be dumb enough to show your faces on the streets."

Her eyes slid to Balor. So, she knew who he was then.

Balor frowned, forehead crinkling. "I see no reason why I shouldn't 'show my face on the street' as you phrased it."

She chuckled before turning to her fellow police

JENNA WOLFHART

officers and jerking a thumb our way. "You hear this shite? This muppet thinks he's done nothing wrong."

When she turned back, her face had transformed into hard, sharp lines. "We know who you are, Balor Beimnech. The old King, or whatever, of the faerie court. The one who killed cops, attacked innocent humans, burned shit down."

I winced. Truth was, some of that had actually happened. The killing the cop thing and attacking innocents? Not so much. But he *had* burned down something. Well, more than one something.

"Erm." The sorcerer, with the book tucked neatly beneath his armpit, gave a little wave of his hand, and then took several steps back. "I'm not with them. We just happened to come out of there at the same time. As you can see, I am very much human. Can I go? Pretty please?"

The officer offered Jake a scowl. "No. Not happening."

Seemed we'd finally found someone he couldn't bribe.

"Okay." He chuckled and gave a slight shake of his head. "Now, don't freak out, okay." And then he cast me a quick look. "Sorry, Clark."

The sorcerer suddenly melted into the night, vanishing from view. A slight breeze as he thundered down the street was the only sign that he'd ever been there.

"Mother fucker," Moira muttered. "Should have seen that one coming."

Unfortunately, the cops before us were not at all amused by the situation. I guessed they weren't used to seeing suspects vanish into thin air.

INNOCENT UNTIL PROVEN FAE

"I thought he said he wasn't a faerie," the lead cop shouted, striding closer with a vein pulsing in her creased forehead. "Where the hell is he?"

"He's not fae," I said. "He's...well, he can do magic. Like invisibility."

"Invisibility." She coughed out a sarcastic laugh and turned to her cop friends, who had both gone white as a sheet. "You can't honestly believe we'd fall for that. Now, where the hell is he?"

"He's gone," Balor said in a low voice. "He vanished. You're welcome to try to find him, but he'll be long gone by now. The coward."

Oh, Jake would never hear the end of this when, or if, we got out of this mess. He was in deep, deep shit.

A moment passed in tense silence. Balor stared at the cops. The cops stared at Balor. I could tell they didn't totally buy our story about Jake, and I didn't blame them. It wasn't every day someone saw a purple-robed lunatic transform from a person-shape into a shadow.

"We aren't interested in him," the cop finally said. "We're here for you and your two accomplices."

Balor arched a brow. "Accomplices to what, exactly?"

"Supernatural harassment," she said in a clipped tone.

I blinked. "Yeah, that's not an actual thing."

"It wasn't an actual thing until yesterday. The Mayor has just instated a new law. No supes on the streets after dark. Supes must abide by any and all bans by human establishments. Breaking said law results in a sentence of anywhere from five years to life. Now, turn around and get on your knees."

A growl emanated from Balor's throat, too low for the humans to hear. All the hair on my arms had stood on end, chills sweeping across the length of me. The humans had finally done it, something we'd long feared would happen. They were singling us out, doing their very best to get every single one of us behind bars.

What they probably didn't understand? Most fae would not go down without a fight.

The cop arched her brow when none of us moved or spoke. "Was there something about what I said that you didn't understand? We're arresting you. Turn around and get on your knees."

I cut my eyes toward Balor and lowered my voice. "Ah, any ideas, boss? If we let them take us to prison, that's it."

"Everything is over," Moira murmured in agreement.

"There's only one thing to do," Balor said. "They don't have guns. I know your speed isn't quite like ours, Clark, but—"

He didn't need to say more. I twisted on my heels and was halfway down the block before the pounding feet of Balor and Moira followed. The shouts of the police echoed off the quiet buildings, their voices ricocheting against the brick and steel. Balor caught up with me in no time. I'd gotten faster these past few months, but never as fast as him.

"Where's Moira?" I puffed out as we spun around another corner, the humans falling even further behind.

"Decided to split up. She'll meet us back at the flat."

Another shout echoed behind us. Casting a glance over my shoulder, I swore and sped up once again. Sirens exploded into the night air, and the sky turned a neon shade of blue. All we could do was keep running.

~

*A*n hour later, Balor and I strode quietly through the East London streets. We'd taken a very winding and twisty path back, anxious the police might be lurking around the corner at every turn. In the end, we'd been too fast for them, though the sirens echoed behind us for far too long.

After climbing the creaking stairs of the building, I stepped inside the open door of the apartment, my hand clutching the shirt fabric near my heart. Someone had well and truly trashed the place, leaving nothing behind but a bunch of rubble. The computers had been taken, along with the maze of papers we'd tacked to the cork board. Only a few small scraps were left behind.

Kyle and Moira were nowhere to be seen. Only her sword had been left behind. It stood to attention just beside the small fridge, the steel winking from the overhead light.

I turned to Balor, heart hammering hard. "She found us. Nemain finally found us."

Two lines had appeared between Balor's eyes as he scanned the room. "I'm not sure she did."

"What do you mean? Of course she did. Look at

the place. You can't honestly believe that someone else did this, can you?"

"If Nemain had found us, she and her Fianna would have been here waiting for us," Balor said, spinning in a circle. "She wants us dead. No, this is the work of someone else."

"But who?" I threw up my hands. "Are you seriously telling me we have another enemy?"

Balor took a long, slow sniff in through flared nostrils. "I am. And whoever it is, they're fae."

13

"We need to find Moira. And Kyle." I paced across shards of broken table, striding from one end of the living room to the other. "She doesn't have her sword with her. She's helpless against whoever attacked this place."

"There are many things I would call Moira, Clark. Helpless is not one of them."

I came to a sudden stop in the middle of the rubble, my boots kicking broken wooden pieces of the table. Propping my fisted hands on my hips, I scowled in Balor's direction. "Stop being so calm. Someone came here and abducted our friends."

His eye flashed. "One moment, you're telling me I need to calm down. The next, you want me to do the opposite. Make up your mind, Clark."

A flickering heat flared through my core, and a familiar feeling came over me. It had been a long time since I'd felt this irritated with Balor Beimnech. Once we'd finally accepted the bond we shared, our once

99

antagonistic relationship had softened into gooey peanut butter rather than knives.

But his insufferable nonchalance in the face of so much pain and fear reminded me exactly why I'd found him so hard to shake in the first place. He knew how to get under my skin. And right now, I wasn't particularly thrilled by it.

I strode over to him and punched my finger into his chest, a move that shot pain through my hand. He flicked his eyes down, bit back a smile.

"Stop acting like I'm some kind of hysterical female," I snapped. "Moira and Kyle are missing. Based on the contents of this flat, they were attacked. I'm all about you controlling your damn temper, but this is not the time to be bloody calm!"

He continued to stare down at me with a blank expression on his face. "Are you done?"

I blew out a hot breath.

"Because you know that I would not allow this kind of conversation with any other fae in the Crimson Court."

"Good thing I am not any other fae, huh?"

"I assume you think I should just let you get away with this," he murmured, stepping closer and narrowing his eyes.

I snorted. "What are you going to do? Punish me?"

"I very well might." He reached around the back of my head and dug his fingers into my hair. And then he squeezed tight, his fist gripping the strands. His power pulsed against my skin, and I gasped, trying to push away that heat that was pressing in around me. My core flickered with a need so great that I could hardly remember the reason he'd made me so mad.

"Insubordination," Balor growled as he twisted me around and pressed me tightly against the wall, "must be punished accordingly."

I nibbled on my bottom lip. "Then, please. Punish me, sir."

With a growl, Balor leapt forward and pinned me to the ground. He angled his body over mine and somehow managed to yank my shirt over my head with one hand. The sound of my passion drowned out everything else.

***

"Who is that?" My closest advisor, Lady Edith, peered over my shoulder at the Squires sparring in the courtyard below. Nemain was one of our strongest. She seemed to anticipate every attack against her before they could knock her off her feet.

"One of my new Squires. She came highly recommended by one of our local farmers. Said she had quite the knack with the sword."

"Hmm." Lady Edith wrinkled her nose. "I have a bad feeling about her."

I laughed. "You have a bad feeling about everyone, Lady Edith."

"The curse of my gift," she merely replied. "No one is trustworthy, therefore everyone is to be feared. Except for you, of course, my Queen."

I cast a sideways glance at my dearest advisor. She had been by my side since the moment I had discovered I was the reincarnated Morrigan, at the bright age of fourteen. Her power was quite useful for a ruler. She could get certain senses about people. Problem was, everyone we met was crooked in one way or another.

JENNA WOLFHART

"Perhaps you can find out something more about this one?" I raised my brows. *"She shows ambition, skill with the blade."*

"Ambition." Lady Edith snorted. *"Since when is that a good thing at Court?"*

"Not everyone is out to get us, dear Edith."

"You are right, of course." She gave a slight bow before turning her gaze back on the courtyard. *"But that one...I am telling you, there is nothing good behind those eyes."*

"Shall we bring her up here so you can get a closer look?"

Edith's face blanched. *"Very well. If you'd like."*

"Good." I gave a satisfied nod, and gave the signal to one of the Knights below. A moment later, our Squire stood before us, all bowed head and clasped hands.

"Hello, Nemain. It looks like you're settling in well. You are quite the little fighter."

Something odd flashed in Nemain's eyes, but her smile hid whatever it had been. *"Thank you, my Queen. I am determined to rise to the top."*

I glanced at Lady Edith who stood frowning at the young fae.

"This is my closest advisor, Lady Edith," I said, waving to my dear friend. *"She has been right by my side since the start of my reign."*

"I know you." Nemain's eyes flashed as she turned to Edith. *"You're the one who can read people's souls. You can tell whether they're dark or light."*

"Something like that," Edith said with a tight smile.

Nemain rolled back her shoulders and stared at Lady Edith straight on. Not many people were willing to do that. *"And what do you see when you look at me?"*

Edith blinked, slowly, as she stared down at the Squire. *"Light, my dear. Of course."*

Nemain tipped back her head and laughed, but it wasn't the

kind of sound that happy people made. It was the kind of sound that felt like ice sinking deep into your bones in the middle of the night. "Of course. What else would I be?"

She turned to me then and smiled. "I would like to get back to training."

"Very well then." I waved at her. "Off you go."

Nemain twirled on her heels and stalked away. I stared after her, pursing my lips. "Lady Edith, do you still feel the same as you felt before?"

"I don't believe I need to answer that, Your Highness. I don't believe I need to answer that at all."

14

I woke up in the middle of the trashed flat with no one to keep me company except for the broken shards of the table. Balor was already up, speaking quietly into his phone. Groaning, I sat up and shielded my eyes against a too-bright sun. How long had we been passed out from our...well, let's just call them *antics*?

We shouldn't have been sleeping. Not with Moira and Kyle out there, taken, abducted, who knew what. Heart hammering, I blinked my eyes and tried to rid my brain of the overwhelming fog of our mating bond. Plus, that dream. I shook my head. Really didn't have the time to think about that right now.

"What time is it?" I asked him.

He frowned and slid the phone into his pocket. "It's late, but you don't need to get up."

Memories of the night before flooded into my mind. The sorcerer club. The vanishing Jake. The human cops. And, worst of all, the disappearance of Moira and Kyle.

JENNA WOLFHART

Quickly, I scrambled to my feet and brushed my fuzzy hair from my eyes. "Moira and Kyle aren't going to save themselves."

Balor pursed his lips and twisted away. A strange unease settled over me. There was something he wasn't telling me. Something he knew I wouldn't like. For the love of the seven, I wished I could read his damn mind.

"Tell me what's going on. Better to rip off the bandaid and get it over with."

He turned back to me, sighed. "Plaster."

I furrowed my brows. "Excuse me?"

"We call them plasters here."

"You're seriously not lecturing me on cultural differences in terminology to avoid sharing information with me, are you?"

He sighed and dragged a hand down his face, fingers snagging on his black eye patch. "I'm meeting Jake in half an hour. He found the appropriate spell. We're going to try it on Maeve."

My heart tripped. "You can't be serious. We don't have time to go practice spells right now. We need to be searching for our friends."

"Sluagh first," he said in a firm, unyielding voice. "Then, we will find the others."

I shook my head and backed away. "I can't believe you're saying that. We have no idea what happened to them. They could be in chains. They might be tortured. Or even worse than that."

"Moira is one of the strongest and most capable fae I've ever met." He shook his head and strode closer to me. "Listen, Clark. I want to go for them just as much as you do. But you saw Maeve. She is already

INNOCENT UNTIL PROVEN FAE

decomposing. If we don't undo the curse now, there will be no way to save her. And we need her to take back the Court."

"*Moira* is the Court. *Kyle* is the Court. They need us."

His eyes fluttered shut. "And so do the rest of my fae. Hundreds of them. They need me to do whatever it takes to make this right."

I shook my head, mouth falling open when he sheathed his sword and strode toward the door. When he reached it, he paused, fingers thrumming against the doorframe. "Are you coming with me?"

"No, I don't think so," I whispered, unshed tears burning my eyes.

With a sigh, he shook his head and disappeared. My heart ached the moment he stepped out of my sight. Everything within me, the very depths of my soul, wanted to rush after him and stay by his side forever. The bond cried out, the magic of our love roiling through me. But I stood my ground. Balor might not want to rescue our friends.

I did.

$\sim$

With a deep breath, I rapped my knuckles against the door. This was the last place I wanted to be, particularly without Balor as backup, but I saw no way around it. For Moira, I would face a nightmare.

The door cracked open, and Henry's whiskery eyes peered out at me. "Hello, love. I thought it might be you."

JENNA WOLFHART

Great. That probably meant he was more than aware the flat had been trashed. Again.

"Sorry to bother you," I said. "I just wanted to ask you a couple of questions, if you don't mind."

"If it's about those youths, then I'm more than happy to oblige. Come in for some tea and a chinwag?"

Huh. Well, that was unexpected. Henry usually tended toward frustrated anger when it came to my unfortunate encounters with destruction-prone supes. I mean, the whole reason I'd been kicked out of the place was because some love-scorned werewolves decided to put some dents in the wall.

(*I* hadn't scorned them. I'd just been the messenger.)

Henry cracked the door open a little wider and motioned me inside. As I cast a glance around his tiny flat, he disappeared through a doorless doorway. I peeked inside to see him fiddling with the kettle and grabbing two mismatched mugs from the cupboard.

He glanced over to me and shouted over the boiling water. "How do you like your tea? Milk and sugar?"

"Sugar, please. No milk."

He gave a nod and then gave me a little wave. "Go make yourself at home. I'll be right out."

I drifted away from the kitchen and down a short hallway. It led to a living room that was even smaller than the one we had upstairs. Unlike mine, Henry's place was absolutely bursting with...well, let's call it *character*.

A faded red and brown rug spread across the hardwood floor while mismatched sofas and armchairs

INNOCENT UNTIL PROVEN FAE

had been crammed around a wooden coffee table covered in dog-eared gardening magazines from the 80's and 90's. The walls were just as crowded. Old faded photographs of a young Henry with his late wife. Framed magazine covers of beautiful flowers. Random artwork that followed no particular theme.

I kind of loved it. His home felt lived in. It felt like it belonged to him. It made my heart ache for that tiny little room I'd had back at the Court. While I'd only lived a few weeks there, a part of my soul had imprinted on the place.

With another glance around at his cluttered, comfortable home, I settled in on one of the sofas.

"Here we are, love." Henry bustled into the living room and handed me a steaming mug that said, "My heart is where my dog is" and then settled into the faded recliner with an audible sigh.

"Thanks," I said, setting the mug on the coaster to give it a moment to cool.

"So, tell me why you're here."

"It sounds like you already know why I'm here."

He gave a slight nod. "Some hooligans got into the building. They targeted your place. I thought about calling the police but then thought better of it. If that Queen of yours has any contacts at Scotland Yard, this might have tipped her off to your location."

I lifted my mug and took a sip of the hot liquid, more to give myself a moment to think than anything else. Henry was being a hell of a lot cooler about this than I'd expected.

"She's not my Queen," I said quietly.

"Ah, yes. Wrong choice of words."

I furrowed my brows. "Why are you being so nice?

JENNA WOLFHART

Why are you even helping us? The last time someone trashed my place, you told me I had to be out of here in a day."

"Things aren't the same now as they were then." He set down his mug and gave me a watery smile. "For one, your lovely man has agreed to pay for the damages. For another, none of the other residents saw. But mainly, whoever those kids were, they weren't anything supernatural. After spending so much time around you, I know what to look out for, and none of them had the shimmer."

I arched a brow. "The shimmer?"

"That's what I like to call it, yes." He gave a nod. "There's something, an aura I guess. It makes you stand out."

I'd certainly never heard that one before, but I wasn't about to argue when he was more than willing to forgive this incident. And it wasn't the most important thing he'd said. "So, you're telling me that *humans* broke into the flat, trashed the place, and stole our computers?"

"That is exactly what I am telling you."

"But...why?" And how had Balor sniffed out a fae? He didn't usually get that kind of thing wrong.

Henry shrugged. "I'm afraid that I don't know. All I know is that they weren't supernatural, and they went into the Corner Express right after. I waited at the window to see what they'd do when they left, but they never came back out the front door."

My ears pricked up, and I sat up a bit straighter. "You saw them go into Corner Express?"

"Oh, yes. There were about five of them."

"Thanks, Henry." I popped up out of the chair. "I

INNOCENT UNTIL PROVEN FAE

appreciate the tea, I really do, but I can't stay to finish it. There's something I have to do."

"Don't forget to take notes about this for your podcast!" he shouted after me.

~

$\mathcal{C}$orner Express wasn't the kind of place I'd ever paid much attention to. It kind of just blended into the block. A small squat of a store that was no different than any of the other thousands of corner shops that were scattered around London. There were as many of them as there were rats.

I'd been in a few times. Once, to buy a pack of Red bulls for a late night of surveillance. Another time to grab a couple of bags of rice, back when I'd been too poor to afford much of anything else.

The door dinged as I pushed inside. The shop made a perfect square. Three aisles in the very center. The far wall held a fridge section full of beer and soda. There wasn't much to it. Just the staples and a few basic food options. The floor looked like it hadn't been mopped in a month, all speckled dirt and crisp crumbs.

Rolling back my shoulders, I strode to the back of the store with all the outward confidence I could muster. One thing I'd learned really quickly, back when I'd first gone on the run all alone. If you act like you know exactly what you're doing, people will rarely question you.

I stopped just inches from a thick black door. If the intruders had come into this shop, this was the only

JENNA WOLFHART

place they could have gone. I tried the doorknob, but it was locked.

"Excuse me? What the hell do you think you're doing?"

I twisted toward the voice. A pimply-faced teen scowled at me from behind the cash register. "You shouldn't be poking around over there."

"Sorry. I thought this might be the toilets."

"That's our stockroom. We don't have toilets." He furrowed his eyebrows. "Besides, I've seen you around. You live in that building across the street. If you need to wee, just go home."

"Great idea. It's just my toilet is broken. You sure you don't have one back there in your stock room? Where do you go if you need a break during your shift?"

"It's not for customers."

I tried on a smile. "Good thing I'm not a customer then. I'm just your friendly neighborhood...neighbor. In desperate need of your facilities."

He blinked at me, glanced around at the empty shop, and then let out a heavy sigh. "Fine. But just this once. And then go get your toilet fixed."

"The plumber is on his way," I said.

He rolled his eyes but scurried on over and unlocked the door for me. "Make it fast."

"No problem. Thanks."

The stockroom was just that. Full of stock. No Moira. No Kyle. And certainly no murderous humans with flashing kitchen knives. It just didn't make any sense. Henry had been certain the intruders had disappeared into this shop and then never came out.

INNOCENT UNTIL PROVEN FAE

And this was the only place they could have gone. There wasn't even a back exit.

With a frustrated sigh, I went into the toilet and hit the flush before running the sink for a moment, partially to give myself some time to think. There had to be some explanation for this, but there wasn't any. Humans can't just...disappear.

"Hey," I said to the cashier when I strode back into the shop. "You didn't happen to be working last night?"

He frowned. "Yeah. I work most shifts. Trying to save up some money. Why?"

"See anything weird? Like some people running around with computers?" I didn't wait for him to answer, just in case he knew these crooks and tried to cover for them. I threw my mind toward him, slipping through his thoughts. There were no boundaries at all, nothing to stop me from reading the avalanche of words.

...see a lot of muppets running around at night...specially in this neighborhood...nothing any weirder than usual...who runs around with computers?

Sucking in a deep breath, I pulled back out of his head to find him staring at me with his head cocked sideways. "Hello? Did you hear me?"

"Sorry, what was that?"

"Said I didn't see anyone running around with any computers. Why? Someone steal yours or something?"

"Yeah," I said. "That's exactly it. If you do happen to see anything, you know where I am."

15

When I pushed open the door to the flat, I knew something was wrong. There was a strange scent in the air, like grass and snow, and magic shimmered beneath the surface airwaves of the world. I glanced around the room, taking a deep breath in through my nose, desperate for Balor's heightened sense of smell.

"Hi." A large form stepped out from the bedroom doorway.

All the breath got sucked from my lungs. For a moment, all I could do was stare. Coal black hair, sharp, pointed ears, cheekbones that could cut like a knife, and thick muscles that stretched his dark t-shirt. The stubble on his jaw had thickened from the last time I'd seen him, and there was a hollowness around his dark eyes that hadn't been there before.

"Tiarnan?" I blinked at the warrior fae who had once sparked desire within me. Now, when I looked at him, all I could see was the betrayal that he'd set upon me and the House. "What are you doing here? I thought you'd left London."

"I did leave. I had to clear my head and distance myself from the Court." He leaned against the wall, muscular arms crossed over his chest. "But I came back when I heard that Nemain had taken control of the Crimson Court."

My heart squeezed tight, and I pressed my sweaty palms against my jeans. "Wow. So, you came back to help your murderous Queen. I don't know why I'm so surprised. You always were on her side."

"No, I wasn't." A frown deepened the creases around his eyes. "I was on *Fionn's* side. My Master's. I was bound to him just as you were to Balor. But he's dead now."

"Yeah, he's dead. So, now you're bonded to Nemain. You'll do whatever she asks of you, even if you don't agree with it." I narrowed my eyes and took a step back. "Of course, you probably agree with each and everything she's done, even the murders. I think you made your loyalty more than clear."

"I am not bonded to her," he said simply. "When I left London, Fionn formally banished me from his House. I'm no longer a member of the Crimson Court, which means I cannot be forced to do a damn thing. My mind is my own, and so are my actions."

This couldn't be real. I couldn't trust him. He'd betrayed me once before, and he'd been driven away from his home because of it. There was no way in hell he was here to help. More likely, he wanted his revenge.

I took another step back, shook my head. "If you

believe that I could trust you, then you're not as smart as I thought you were."

I needed to get out of here. Moira and Kyle were still out there, somehow. Staying here and arguing with the enemy wouldn't help them. It wouldn't help anyone.

As I turned to go, he cleared his throat. "You want to find your friends, don't you? Kyle and Moira, I believe are their names."

I whirled back to face him, fisted hands shaking by my sides. "Where are they? What have you done with them?"

"Relax." He held up his hands. "They're fine. Some sorcerers showed up here last night. There was a scuffle, as you can see. The sorcerers fled with the computers, and Moira and Kyle went after them. Moira seemed pretty livid. I'd worry more about the sorcerers than anything else."

"Wait." I blinked, trying to make sense of his words. "You're saying that *sorcerers* did this?"

"Yes, some strange looking ones, in fact. The leader seemed to be a girl wearing a red cape."

I pressed my lips tightly together. "That would be Elena. She gave us a spell book we needed. I have no idea why she would do something like this."

He lifted a shoulder in a shrug. "Perhaps she wanted her spell book back."

"No. She wouldn't have taken the computers if that was what she was after." I frowned. "But more importantly, why were *you* here, Tiarnan? How do you know all of this?"

He had the decency to look the slightest bit ashamed. "Ah. Well. I was trying to track you down. I listened to your old podcasts for clues and managed to find the place. I was going to wait for you to show up, but decided I shouldn't be here when you found it trashed."

"Yeah, you're not wrong about that," I mumbled.

"So." He shifted in his boots. "Where is your mate?"

My cheeks flushed with heat. "He's taking care of something else...how did you know? About the mating thing?"

"I can sense it. You look...different. More alive." He let out a heavy sigh. "It suits you."

My hands formed fists. When I'd first met Tiarnan, we'd had an instant connection. Obviously, I'd suspected he might be the fae behind the attacks on Balor's Court, but he proved himself to me. We'd fought side by side. We'd been a team. Until I'd learned that he'd only gotten close to me on his Master's orders.

"Look, Tiarnan. I appreciate the heads-up, but I don't know if we can—I just...why did you try to come and find me?"

He pressed away from the wall and paced the length of the room. Then, suddenly, he stopped. "You won't believe me."

I arched a brow. "Probably not, but I'll hear you out. Why have you come back to London?"

His eyes met mine, dark and full of pain. "I made a mistake. I did some things I shouldn't have, and I said some terrible things. It was all wrong, and I just...well, I'm sorry."

My heart thumped hard in my chest. I could scarcely believe the words coming out of Tiarnan's

INNOCENT UNTIL PROVEN FAE

mouth. When Fionn had been wrestling for control over the Court, Tiarnan had proven himself to be just as hate-filled against shifters as Nemain. And that was only the cherry on top of the whole betrayal thing.

"If you want me to forgive you, you're going to have to do better than some half-assed apology, one only given to me after you stalked me through the streets."

He strode across the room and placed warm and steady hands on my shoulders, dipping his head low so that he could stare right into my eyes, and my soul. "I know what I did hurt you. It would have hurt me, too. But I want you to know that I did not get to know you just because Fionn wanted me to. I won't lie and say that wasn't a part of it, because it was. But it was more than that. You and me...we had our own kind of bond, a connection. I know you're mated now, but you can't deny that was the truth."

Softly, I pushed against his chest. "We *had* a connection. And then you fucked it up."

This was insane. With a deep breath, I paced from one end of the debris-covered floor to the other, trying and failing to wrap my head around this newest development. Tiarnan was here. And he was no longer bound to the Court.

Of course, he could be lying.

I frowned and glanced up at him. His gaze was steady and clear, and his lips twitched as he gave me a resigned smile. "I know what you're thinking, Clark. You want to read my mind to find out the truth. Well, go on then. Do it if you must."

"You understand why, right?" I asked. "The last time I took you at your word..."

"I get it, Clark."

Tiarnan hated having his mind read. So did most people, actually. But this was far too big for me to chance. I'd avoided it when we first met because I'd wanted to trust him. He'd tried to whisk me off my feet, woo me in order to find out more of Balor's plans. I could never forget that he'd gone so far as to pretend he wanted me.

"Think about your bond with Nemain. Think about your intentions for coming here." I delved into his mind. At first, there was a little push back. Even though he'd willingly agreed to be read, that didn't change his instinctual reaction to someone digging around inside of his thoughts.

But I pushed and pushed, and his walls slowly fell away.

I came here because I want to make things right...Nemain is not to be trusted...violent...cunning...

I breathed through my nose as I forced myself to stay inside of his mind, my eyes watering as I stared straight into the very center of his thoughts. "Are you bonded to Nemain?"

No. I am bonded to no one.

Satisfied, I pulled out of his head. He stood leaning heavily against the wall, his eyebrows pinched tightly together. "You know, I bloody hate that."

"Good," I said. "Maybe next time you think about betraying someone's trust, you'll remember that there are consequences for everything you do."

He let out a soft chuckle. "Trust me, Clark. I could never forget, because you wouldn't let me."

"Yeah, I won't." Sighing, I crossed my arms. "So, what'll it be?"

INNOCENT UNTIL PROVEN FAE

His eyebrows winged upward. "What will what be?"

"You came here to help. What's our next step?"

"Track down those sorcerers and get your friends back."

16

A part of me was glad for the help. Another part of me still wasn't sure I should be teaming up with the guy who had stuck his knife in my back. Problem was, Balor was gone, and I had no one else. I could handle a fight with some sorcerers alone, but even I had to admit that some backup would help.

"You said this happened last night?" Frowning, I paced over to the window and peered outside. Of course, there was nothing to see there. Nothing but a big brick wall that blocked any and every path forward from here.

"Yep," Tiarnan said. "Not long before you and Balor showed up."

I arched a brow and whirled toward him, blood rushing into my face. "You were here for that?"

"I saw you go into the building. That's when I decided it was best I leave."

"And you didn't think to go after Moira and Kyle?"

"I wanted to speak to you first. Besides, they were

JENNA WOLFHART

the ones doing the chasing, not the other way around."

I sighed and slumped against the creaking window-frame. "That was hours ago. There's been no sign of them since, and neither one of them are answering their cells. Moira even left without her sword. I'm worried about them."

"Then, let's go track them down." Tiarnan gave a nod and strode over to the open door of the flat. He paused just as he stepped one foot into the hallway, shooting a glance over his shoulder with raised brows. "You coming?"

≈

On the pavement outside of the building, I explained what Henry had told me about the sorcerers. "You see anything like that?"

"Can't say I did." He pointed in the opposite direction of the shop. "I saw everyone running that way."

"So, what do we do? They could be anywhere."

He rolled back his shoulders, scanned the streets. "I know of a place where sorcerers hang out. That might be a good place to start."

"Infinity? That's where I met them, so they know we have the address. You think they're dumb enough to go back there after stealing our computers?"

"Oh, so you know the place." Tiarnan gave a slow nod. "I think someone there will know something, even if the sorcerers who stole from you aren't there. We might not find all the answers, but we should find something."

"That's good enough for me."

Tiarnan grabbed a motorbike he'd parked across the street, tossing me a helmet. My eyebrows flew up to my hairline as he straddled the seat and cranked the engine, so at ease that it was as if he'd done this a hundred times.

I strode over to him and hopped on the back, sliding across the smooth leather. "Since when did you take up motorbikes? Don't tell me you've joined the Pack."

He let out a low chuckle and revved the engine. "My days were pretty boring when I left the Court. Had to find another way to spend my time. This suited me just fine."

Without another word, Tiarnan pulled the bike away from the curb and shot down the street. A sharp cry flew from my lips, and I was forced to wrap my arms around his waist to cling on. The wind shot against my face. The ground beneath me twisted this way and that.

Moments later, Tiarnan pulled the bike back up to the curb and cut the engine. Every single cell in my face had been stung by the cool air, but I felt alive, exhilarated. I kind of got why people made such a big deal about bikes.

I hopped off and tossed him the helmet. "I see what happened now. You had a midlife crisis."

He let out a low chuckle. "Fae don't get midlife crises but nice try. Our lives are long. Our years plenty. No need to fear the certain end of our youth when there is none."

"Cheesy philosophy, too." I grinned. "You're just full of surprises."

JENNA WOLFHART

"The cheesiness of my philosophy, unfortunately, is not new. You would have found that out if you'd..." He fell silent, and cleared his throat.

The smile died from my lips. "If I'd what? Stuck around? Last time I checked, *you* were the pretender. Not me. I would have never had the chance to leave because it was always going to happen the way it did."

The corners of his eyes turned down. "You're never going to forgive me, are you?"

"I can forgive you enough to bring you on a mission with me. That's saying a hell of a lot after what you did." I pressed my lips tightly together. "But I don't know if I'll ever be able to forget. You broke my trust, something that is hard as hell to earn back."

"That's fair."

He strode away from his bike and came to a stop beside me on the pavement, turning his attention on the hidden cave entrance. It looked a lot different in the daylight. The curved hulking form that popped up out of the ground looked more like something you'd find as an amusement park ride than as the home for a gothic magical club. Rubbish was strewn everywhere, lottery tickets flittering across the petrol-stained ground.

"I can see why it's closed during the day." I wrinkled my nose. "Is that piss I smell?"

"Probably best not to find out." Tiarnan led the way to the steel grey, nondescript door and jiggled the knob. Locked, of course. But Tiarnan slid a tiny pin from his pocket, and a moment later, we were inside.

Our footsteps echoed all around us as we made our way deeper into the caves. There was an eerie silence that hung all over us, along with a dark expansive nothingness. Some torches flickered on the walls. Other than that, this place had been deserted until the crowd piled in later that night.

"They're not here." I came to a stop just at the edge of the roped VIP section where Elena and her friends had been camped out the night before. Spreading my arms, I turned in a full circle. "This place is a dead end."

"We should check out the rest of the place, just to be sure," he said, pointing at the hidden entrance where Elena had disappeared for her spell book. With a shrug, I led the way, ducking behind a thick black tapestry that covered the entrance to the next cave.

"Oh, look. We have visitors." Elena stepped out of the shadows, smiling. "Surprised you would be dumb enough to come here."

I stiffened and reached for my sword. Her eyes flicked down to the pommel, and she tsked. "Careful. I have weapons on your friends. Leave your sword in the sheath. Or we'll kill them."

Horror shook through me as I caught a sudden movement out of the corner of my eye. In the back left corner of the cave, both Moira and Kyle had been tied to twin wooden chairs. Ropes were around each wrist and ankle. A thick white cloth had been stuck into their mouths. Eyes wide, they wiggled on their chairs, desperately trying to escape. Twin blades were pressed against their necks, fellow sorcerers standing guard.

My heart flipped over itself ten thousand times, and my voice was rough when I spoke. "Let them go."

"No can do, I'm afraid. We *need* them."

"You need them?" I frowned. "What the hell for?"

JENNA WOLFHART

A slight smile turned up the corners of her lips. "Jakey boy gave me an idea. He's bending over backwards going out of his way to help you faeries, just so he can get a vampire to turn him into one of them. Well, you know as well as I do, that he probably won't survive. Shame, really. Immortality is where it's at."

A sense of dread settled over my tired bones. "Why do I have the feeling I'm not going to like where you're going with this."

Her smile widened. "So, I thought to myself, surely vampirism isn't the only way to achieve immortality. Faeries are immortal, after all. Thing is, faeries can't turn other people into faeries. But do you know what sorcerers can do? Extract and consume the magic of another living soul. Unfortunately...whoever's soul is extracted...well, dies."

My stomach twisted tight.

"That's insane," Tiarnan muttered.

"Who is this little snack?" Elena sashayed over, red cloak floating around her hips. She poked a long fingernail at his chest, and then dragged it down his tight black shirt. Tiarnan's expression remained impassive, but I spotted the tiny shudder that went through him. "I certainly wouldn't mind consuming *your* soul, that's for damn sure."

Tiarnan slowly reached up, wrapped his fingers around her hand, and then dropped it. "Unfortunately for you, my soul is not available for consumption."

Her sparkling eyes went wicked. "We'll see about that."

She lifted her hands in the air and screamed.

The world went black.

INNOCENT UNTIL PROVEN FAE

"My Queen." Nemain walked up to my throne and knelt before me. She kept her gaze focused on my feet, her hair cascading around her face. "I have just learned we are going to war. The Knights were spinning such stories about it at dinner this evening. Is this true, Your Grace?"

I cocked my head, frowned. Nemain was merely a Squire. She should be serving the Knights, not breaking bread with them. "It is true, though I hope you have not come here to question me about it. I know you have a tendency to want to get involved."

Indeed, she did. I knew not every Squire's name. Nemain had a habit of popping up, often at the most inopportune moments. Some said her power was a sixth kind of sense. I was almost inclined to believe them.

"Of course not." She bowed her head lower. "I just...well, I have been serving as a Squire for many years now. I have spent many hours training and learning. I think I would be an asset if I were given...more responsibilities."

Surprise flickered through me. "You wish to become a Knight."

"I do."

Interesting. Nemain had always struck me as more of a politician than a fighter, but the truth was, we needed fighters on the field. The battle ahead would be very bloody. If she felt ready, then so be it.

"Find a Knight who can confirm your training to me. And then you will get what you wish."

Nemain peered up at me then, and smiled. "I have no doubt I will get exactly what I wish."

17

Fear hurtled through me, and I jumped to my feet, sucking in lungfuls of air. Only, I didn't jump up. Because I was tied to a damn chair. For a moment, I tried to hold onto my dream. Dreams I was quickly beginning to understand weren't dreams at all. They were blinding visions of the past, of when Knights roamed the hills and horses trotted from east to west.

Not that it meant anything. I *wasn't* the Morrigan, regardless of whatever was happening to me. Maybe she was just trying to communicate with me from beyond the grave. Through dreams.

Made total sense.

"Hi," Tiarnan said from beside me. I turned to find him just as tied to a chair as I was, but Elena had left the rag out of his mouth.

I glowered at him.

"Not my fault." He grinned. "She just finds me so irresistible, she couldn't bear to give me the 'ole sock treatment."

Ew. I wrinkled my nose.

"Sorry. I guess that wasn't the right choice of words."

You could say that again.

"So, listen." He cleared his throat. "Got any bright ideas on how to get us out of here? I don't think we have long before they get back. They left to go sell the computers on the black market. So…don't think we're getting those back. Sorry."

I do, actually.

Closing my eyes, I thought about my bird. My limbs twisted and turned, forming wings instead of arms and legs. My nose and mouth stretched out into a beak, and feathers took the place of my skin.

A moment later, I hopped around the chair, no longer bound. The only problem was, I'd totally destroyed my clothes in the shift, and I didn't have a spare set. Oh well. Something to worry about later.

Quickly, I changed back into my fae form and fought back the blush that threatened to creep up on my neck. I was buck naked. In front of Tiarnan. And also Kyle and Moira.

"So, I think I'm just going to untie everyone, and we'll get the hell out of here, okay?" I glanced around. "The computers aren't here. We'll just cut our losses, right?"

Kyle murmured around his sock, but I hushed him quick enough. "This is incredibly humiliating, and I'm saving your asses. We're leaving now, and I won't hear any argument against it."

INNOCENT UNTIL PROVEN FAE

*A*fter I got everyone untied, I changed back into a bird until we passed a shop where I could grab a cheap pair of jeans. Everyone was silent on the trek back, probably out of second-hand embarrassment. I was relieved when we finally reached my street. As we slowed to a stop outside of my flat, a form slid out of the shadows. "Hi, tiny bird."

I blinked, sucking a deep breath as I quickly glanced at Tiarnan. He'd rolled back his shoulders and puffed out his chest, clearly trying to come across the taller of the two. It wasn't working. Tiarnan might be a tall, powerful fae, but Ronan? He was a beast of a wolf, towering, thick, and rugged as hell.

I wet my lips, silently thanking the seven that Balor wasn't here to witness this little reunion. "What the hell are you doing here?"

"Nice to see you, too." He slung his hands into his pockets and rocked back onto the heels of his faded black boots."Glad to see you haven't changed even a little."

"I don't know what you expected," I said dryly. "We needed you. And you left."

"Ouch," Tiarnan said with a chuckle, body slightly relaxing. "Trust me, mate. She's going to hold that over you until the end of the earth."

I merely shot Tiarnan a glare.

"See?" He jerked his thumb in my direction. "We're in the same boat, mate. I feel like I should take you out for a pint so we can commiserate."

"Erm," Kyle said, slowly edging past us. "I'm going to go inside and see what I can recover from the burglary."

"Yeah, I think I'll go with." Moira awkwardly scuttled by and disappeared into the front door of the building.

"Traitors," I muttered before letting out a heavy sigh and turning back toward Ronan. "Seriously, what are you doing here? Thought you said the Pack was done with London, at least until things have shaken out. Well, they haven't."

He crossed his arms over his beefy chest and gave Tiarnan a once-over. "Who's this guy?"

"I'm Tiarnan."

Ronan's face clouded over, and he barked out a laugh. "You shitting me? Seriously? After what he did to you, you're just going to go waltzing around East London with him? In the middle of the night?"

"It's a long story," I said quietly.

"I made a mistake," Tiarnan said with a shrug. "I'm here to make up for it and help win the city back."

The anger vanished from Ronan's face. "Huh. Kind of stole my thunder there, mate. That's what I was going to say to her."

Power rippled through the empty street, and every hair on the back of my neck stood on end. My breath caught, and a strange heat spread through my core. Shit, shit, shit. I flicked my eyes from Tiarnan to Ronan and tried to shake my head in warning but it was no use.

Balor was back.

And he was...*kiiiiiind* of pissed to see them both standing by my side.

Tiarnan stiffened before Ronan did, clearly sensing that something was off.

INNOCENT UNTIL PROVEN FAE

"Get away from her." Balor strode from the shadows to stand just before me, blocking my body from the two males. "I don't know why you're here or what you think you're going to do to her, but you'll have to get through me first. I may have lost my fiery eye, but I am still one hell of a fighter. You'll have to kill me first."

I wrapped my hand around his arm and squeezed tight, though a thrill went through me at the sight of my mate springing in to protect me at all cost. "Balor. Calm down. They're not here to do anything other than help."

He stayed in place, body trembling with rage and need and desperation. I felt the same with every breath I took. "I don't understand. Tiarnan betrayed us both. Ronan ran from a fight we desperately needed to win. Surely you aren't saying you trust them after all of that?"

"No, that's not what I'm saying at all," I said quietly, doing my best to calm my mate's instinctual need to fight. "But they have both come here, trying to make things right. Ronan really isn't one to lie, and I read Tiarnan's mind. He's being sincere."

Balor flicked his eye up and down my body. "Then, why are you wearing *different clothes*?"

I winced. "Maybe we can talk about this inside."

"You two." He slid his finger from one male to the other. "Wait out here. If you step inside that flat, I swear to the seven—"

"Sorry," I mouthed as I dragged Balor away from the street.

18

"Why are they here?" Balor stalked from one end of the flat to the other. Moira and Kyle were hiding out in the bedroom while we had our little shouting match. Hopefully, they were getting some rest, though Balor's quickly rising voice would probably see to it that they weren't.

"Like I told you, they've both come back to make amends."

He narrowed his eyes. "Strange coincidence, don't you think? Both of your exes showing up here at the same damn time?"

I snorted. "Hold up. First, I wouldn't call either of them an *ex*. Second, what are you even suggesting? That a shifter and a banished fae have teamed up to trick me into trusting them? So that...what, exactly? What would be the point of that?"

"Nemain could be behind it, trying to root us out."

"If Nemain knew where we were, she would just come here and kill us."

A beat passed. He knew he couldn't argue with

that, as much as he wanted to. Instead, he turned his fiery attention onto something else. "I see Moira and Kyle made it back in one piece."

"Yep. Tiarnan helped me find them. Turns out, the sorcerers lured them out of the flat and then used some zappy magic on them to knock them out. Know what they're after?"

Balor's eye flickered with darkness. "Wait a minute. Go back a step. You went after the sorcerers *by yourself*? And you took *Tiarnan* with you? I thought we agreed to wait. You could have gotten yourself killed."

"I can't talk to you when you're like this."

"I could say the same damn thing to you."

Sparks of magic jumped from my skin to his and back again. Tendrils of white hot anger and passion swirled between us. That strange, twisted cloud rumbled beneath our feet. Eyes wide, I glanced down, glad for a distraction from our fight.

As soon as I set eyes on it, the dark clouds dispersed into nothing but black flecks of ash.

"Our mating bond," Balor said. "It's making you not think straight."

I jerked up my head, coughed out a laugh. "Me? You're the one who isn't thinking straight."

When his eye caught mine, that white hot need stole over me once again, and it was all I could do to stand my ground. God, everything within me just wanted to run to him and jump into his arms, forget about the fight. Or relish in it. The anger only made me want him that much more, to scratch my fingernails down his back, to...

I shook my head and threw out those thoughts. *Focus.*

INNOCENT UNTIL PROVEN FAE

"Look," I said, holding up my hands. "I know this whole thing is a bit weird. And awkward. But I can promise you, they both mean what they say. They're here to help. And we could use them..."

Frowning, I trailed off, just now realising that I hadn't noticed Jake's absence with all the tense commotion of Balor getting back. "Where's the sorcerer?"

"Ah." Balor winced. "He's gone home. His job was done."

"So, he cured the Sluagh? Why didn't you bring Maeve back here? She shouldn't be staying in some catacomb now that she's no longer a member of the walking dead."

"The Sluagh were gone," he said quietly.

I blinked at him. "What do you mean they were gone?"

"Maeve and the two others weren't in the catacombs when we arrived. We searched all around the cemetery grounds and even waited for awhile to see if they'd come back." A beat passed. "But they were long gone. No sight of them."

Closing my eyes, I let out a heavy sigh and leaned back against the wall. Things were rapidly going from bad to worse. We needed the Sluagh to get some damn allies for once. But what was worse, we could now confirm that man-eating zombies were walking amongst the human population of London. There was no telling how many innocents they would kill before they got their fill.

"We need to do something," I said.

"Agreed. We need to do whatever it takes to find

JENNA WOLFHART

Maeve. Kyle is going to try to get his station set up again so he can hack into CTTV."

"All the computers were stolen, and we couldn't find them at Infinity."

"There's a whole new set of them on the way," he said with a slight smile. "I can't wait to see the look on Kyle's face when he sees."

"Good. We can use them to figure out a way to break into the Court."

Immediately, the smile vanished from Balor's face. "I can't believe you're suggesting that right now. And, let me guess, you want to take your two exes along with you."

"Actually." I propped my fists on my hips. "I do. We need allies. The sorcerers have turned against us. The vamps won't help. And the humans have gone absolutely mad. They're the only two people in this damn city willing to join our cause."

The churning sea of dark magic had returned again. It was hot against my skin, pulsing electric energy that almost burned. Kyle stepped out of the bedroom and widened his eyes.

The next few moments passed in a strange blur. One second, everything was fine. The next, Kyle was flipping through the air. The magic swarmed around him and threw him across the room.

He fell with a thump against the wall.

My heart thundered in my ears as I ran toward him. I fell to his side, my knees digging into the hardwood. "Oh my god, Kyle. Are you okay?"

"Move aside. Let me get a look at him."

I glared up at Balor. "It was your magic that did this."

INNOCENT UNTIL PROVEN FAE

"Mine?" Balor barked out a bitter laugh. "I've lived a long-ass time, love, and my magic has never done this. I'd say it isn't me who is the problem."

Glaring, I jumped to my feet and stormed to the door. Moira awkwardly watched from the bedroom as I threw myself out of the flat. I couldn't talk to Balor like this. I couldn't be around him when the darkest part of our magic made me want to scream. It had just hurt someone we care about. If we kept this up, who would we hurt next?

I had to get out of there.

19

"You okay?" Moira asked as we strode down the steps. I paused in the building's lobby, trying to get a handle on the intense emotions that were giving me whiplash. "You and Balor seem to be..."

"Fighting?" I wrapped my hand around my sword's hilt and squeezed tight, hoping it would help me feel grounded. Instead, it only heightened my need to punch the wall. "You're not wrong. We are definitely fighting."

"Sure, but it seems fuelled by more than just anger." She flicked her golden eyes back and forth across my face. "Honestly, Clark. It's like you're both possessed and can't help yourselves."

"It's the bond," I said, letting out a heavy sigh. "It's making us both go mad. My whole body feels tense. My heart feels like it's about to explode. I'm telling you, I could really use a gin right about now."

"I've seen mating bonds make fae emotional, but

I've never seen it quite as bad as this," she said. "Are you sure it's not more than that?"

My heart pulsed. I hadn't told anyone about the weird cloud thing that had appeared in the alley, and then again in the flat when we'd argued. Kyle knew he was looking into something strange, but he didn't know it had anything to do with the bond. Well, I guessed now he might get the picture. I was almost scared to tell Moira, for fear that she'd confirm my worst suspicions: there was something off, something wrong about the two of us together.

"I think my bond with Balor might be...messed up."

She arched a brow. "Hmm, I wondered. Messed up how?"

I tried to explain to Moira what had happened, but I stumbled over my words. Dark clouds, weird mist, strange energies. I sounded like some kind of conspiracy theorist, even I realised that. But as strange as I felt explaining it, the reality of it had been even stranger.

"Yeah, *that* is not what happens in a mating bond." She shook her head, furrowing her brows. "Maybe it has something to do with the Morrigan."

"Not this again."

"Come on, Clark," she said, throwing her hands in the air. "At this point, you have to admit that there is *something* going on there. Have you had any more of those visions?"

"Dreams." I stiffened. "Yeah, I've had two more. Both of them focused on Nemain. Neither of them had anything to do with a weird magic cloud."

"Right." She nodded. "There's clearly something

INNOCENT UNTIL PROVEN FAE

going on, and it must be important, or it wouldn't keep happening. Don't hate me, but I agree with Balor. We need to take you to see Caer and ask her to tell you the straight, blunt truth of it all."

Going to see Caer was the last thing in the world I wanted to do. Hell, I'd even rather take a bath in the Thames and wear the stink of the river on me for seven days straight. The Goddess of Prophecies had been seeing so many other people's future lives that her own had started to melt away. Reality and Caer did not get along. And she was not a fan of visitors.

Not to mention...I was more than a little scared to hear what she'd have to say about my link with the Morrigan.

With a deep breath, I stepped forward and placed my hands on my best friend's shoulders. "How about this? I will go see Caer and ask her to tell me the full truth about the Morrigan but only after everything is back to normal. After we're back in the Court, after Nemain has been deposed, after the city is at peace again."

She let out a laugh and shook her head. "Alright, Clark. We'll make that a deal, but don't think I didn't notice that last bit. I doubt the city will ever be at peace again."

Truth be told, I had a hard time believing it myself.

～

*R*onan and Tiarnan fell silent when we stepped foot on the pavement. I was pretty sure they'd been talking about me, which didn't make

145

JENNA WOLFHART

me feel particularly thrilled, I guess you could say. While I'd insisted neither was an ex, they both kind of were in their own way. Tiarnan and I had a brief moment where we'd been dating. And Ronan and I? Well, things had gotten a little heated in the old warehouse where we'd once lived.

And to think they were now out here comparing notes? Yeah, not a fan.

"Everything all good now?" Ronan lifted a thick brow, glanced behind me at the door falling shut behind us. "Or has Balor ordered us to leave?"

"He doesn't want you here, but I do," I said as matter-of-factly as I could without letting the riptide of emotion flood through my voice.

Ronan cocked his head. "You two sure do have one hell of a mating bond. You smell like twin stars about to crash into each other."

That was one way to put it.

I opened my mouth to argue, but Moira jumped in before I could.

"Enough about that. We've decided that we'd like to enlist your help in taking back the Court. Right, Clark?" Moira said in a chirpy voice that sounded nothing like her matter-of-fact blunt self.

I gave a nod. "Damn straight. London has reached boiling point. The fae stuck inside that building are all in danger. It's time we did something instead of running around the streets like headless chickens."

Ronan nodded and rocked back on his heels. "I'm listening. The Pack are scattered all across the country. Half went north, half went further south. They're stronger, safer, when they're all together. But they can't come back to London until Nemain is gone."

INNOCENT UNTIL PROVEN FAE

I turned to Tiarnan. "This is your last chance to bail."

"I said I'm in. So, I'm in."

～

*A*cross the river, the four of us sat on a docked boat that had been transformed into a local watering hole. It rocked gently on the water, a cool wind blowing at the edges of the small, square napkins underneath our pint glasses. Well, everyone else's pint glasses. I'd opted for a double gin and tonic. After the past week and the night we surely had ahead, I needed the soothing liquid.

Ronan drummed his knuckles on the table, frowning. "I can't help but notice you brought us to a bar right across the river from your old haunt."

I glanced to the left, drinking in the tall, towering expansive building that had once been the Battersea Power Station. The front of it had been transformed while we'd been gone. At one point in time, it had been a burned out husk, but now it displayed floor to ceiling windows so that gawkers could see the curving stairs and the sparkling chandeliers inside.

"Surveillance is one of the most important aspects of the job. As you can see, we've got two guards stationed at the front. There are some security cameras mounted up along the front path as well." I shrugged and smiled. "If we hadn't done a bit of a stake-out, we wouldn't know that information, now would we?"

Tiarnan's face clouded over. "And why exactly are we gathering information about Nemain's security protocols? You don't actually expect us to go charging in there, do you?"

I nibbled on my bottom lip in response.

Ronan's mouth dropped open. He pounded a fist on the table and leaned forward. "You said nothing about a suicide mission."

"It's not a suicide mission if we're prepared. That's why we scope things out. Take a look around. See what we're up against."

Tiarnan growled. "What we're up against is a whole army. The Fianna. There's dozens of them and four of us. We don't stand a chance against them."

"You can help us with that," I said. "You spent your entire life training with them, fighting beside them. You know strategies and how they think and move. That will give us a bit of an edge."

"This is insanity," Ronan muttered before downing his beer in one gulp.

I sighed and glanced to Moira who hadn't spoken a word since we'd sunken into the booth on the starboard end of the boat. "Back me up here, Moira."

She winced, fingering the wooden grooves before her. "Thing is, they're not wrong here, Clark. The whole reason you, me, and Balor haven't gone in already is because we just don't have the manpower. We need allies. More fighters."

"Look." I turned to look at each one of them in turn. "I'm not asking you to run inside with swords raised high. The reason we scope things out? So that we know how to get in and out without being seen. It will also help us plan for the full-on attack that we're going to do. Just...later. Once this whole Maeve thing shakes out."

INNOCENT UNTIL PROVEN FAE

Ronan furrowed his brows. "I don't understand. Why are we sneaking into the Crimson Court *now*? What the hell kind of good will that do?"

I flicked my eyes to Moira, and realisation dawned in her eyes. "Our friend is in danger. She's been taken into the dungeons, and Nemain knows she's valuable. It's only a matter of time before Nemain takes her rage out on Elise."

"You want to break her out of there," Moira said in a whisper, a shiny gloss covering her eyes. "You don't want to sneak into the Court to kill Nemain. You want to save Elise."

"Exactly." I stabbed my finger into the table. "But if I do get a chance at Nemain? I'm fucking taking it."

20

We did a little more reconnaissance work before making our move. We camped out all night near the Court, keeping an eye on the guard rotation. When the boat bar shut down, we settled in on a bench a little further down the river's edge. Finally, when the moon was high in the sky, I stood from the bench and brushed off my jeans.

"We should make our move now before daylight." I pulled my phone from my pocket and shot off a text. If we were going to do this, we'd need a little more help.

"We won't be able to go through the front," Ronan said, taking a spot by my side. It was strange working beside him once again. We'd left things so uncomfortably awkward when he'd fled London. I didn't know how to talk about what had happened between us, but I also didn't know how *not* to talk about it.

"Thanks for coming back, by the way," I whispered up to him. "I honestly thought I'd never see you again."

"You probably would have preferred it that way, eh?" He chuckled, but I could hear a hint of pain behind the smile.

"Nah. You're a pain most of the time, but you grew on me. Like a wet barnacle." I looked up and grinned.

He snorted. "Right back at you, tiny bird."

"I'm serious," I said, smile dimming. "I mean, I'm still pissed off at you for running, especially since we totally failed at winning the fight against Nemain. But I don't hate you. I never did. If I didn't think it would give you an even bigger ego, I might go as far as saying that I kind of like your company. Sometimes. Like I said, wet barnacle."

"You just like Balor's company more," he said softly.

My heart clenched tight. I couldn't think about Balor, not right now, even though we were five minutes away from storming into his Court. The last few days had been a knife digging into my heart and twisting tight. We'd only just finally come together as mates, and now it felt as though we were being yanked apart violently. The arguments, the anger, that strange dark cloud that had ripped through the flat and wounded Kyle.

All I wanted was for things to go back to how they'd been, only a few days ago. I wanted to look at him and see my future, to see the years of happiness stretching out before us.

"The relationship I have with Balor is complicated. It always has been." I gave him a tight smile. "You know that."

"Sometimes the ones who love us the most are also

INNOCENT UNTIL PROVEN FAE

the ones who hurt us the most." He let out a heavy sigh and crossed his arms. I knew where his mind had gone in that moment. Back to when his Pack had been brutally ripped away from him. The Fianna had done that.

"Remember, not all fae hate shifters."

He inclined his head toward the Court. "The ones in that building do. The ones in charge, at least."

"Not for long," I whispered. It was a promise. One that I would keep.

◈

I flapped my wings as I lowered myself into the courtyard. When I landed, I perched on top of a Morrigan statue, settling in to scan the garden with my beady little eyes. The world whirled in strange colours and shapes. The trees were larger. The chirping birds were louder. Everything was enhanced to a thousand degrees.

For a long moment, I waited. The guards, at least when I'd been one, had never stationed themselves in the courtyard. There'd never been a need. Sure, we did our nightly patrol through the grounds, just to make sure that everyone was safe and sound. But there was no way to get in here except through the actual building of the Court.

And the sky.

In the back left corner, a door opened and shut. A hooded figure scurried through the winding paths, casting quick glances from beneath the black cotton. After a moment, her gaze seemed to settle on the Morrigan statue.

153

JENNA WOLFHART

"Is that you?" Ondine hissed when she came to a stop on the path just in front of me. She pushed back her hood, scanning my bird form with wide eyes. "Or am I just talking to a bird like a bloody idiot?"

I couldn't really answer her. Birds don't talk, after all. Instead, I gave a little flap of my wings and chirped.

"Right. I'm going to take that as confirmation, even though I feel absolutely ridiculous." She held out the crook of her elbow, sighed. "Go on then. Climb on."

I hopped off the statue and onto Ondine's arm. With a furtive glance all around, she scurried back to the door from whence she'd come.

The plan was this: Ondine would get me inside, and I would stay in bird form as long as possible. She was scared of getting caught, and I couldn't blame her. Not to mention, she couldn't realistically be caught in the same room with Moira without being forced to run off and tell Nemain.

Once I was safely inside and no one was around, I'd shift and let the others in through the back door.

Easy peasy.

Ondine pushed open the door to the Court and strode inside. The door clicked shut behind us, and I let out a slight sigh. Getting inside had felt like the hardest part of it all, and here I was. Back inside my home once again.

Wings twitching, I glanced around. Nothing looked at all different, yet it felt nothing like the Court it had once been. The thin hallway stretched out before us on either side, leading to the various wings. The left would lead us to the lobby and the staircase that led up to the residential part of the building. The right would lead to the luxurious restaurant. Further down, we'd find the old command station. Had the Fianna taken up residence there?

Footsteps echoed on the floor, and Ondine turned to find Emma striding away from the restaurant, her arm tucked into the elbow of Oscar. Her smile dimmed, alarm flickering across her pixie features. "What do you have there?"

"Oh, this?" She let out a nervous laugh. "Found it in the courtyard, and it couldn't seem to fly away. I thought I'd see if one of the healers could take a look. Late night?"

Not bad.

Oscar grinned. "Luckily, the restaurant is open twenty-four seven. Even though it's way past midnight, this one was starving."

"A raven?" Emma's frown deepened. "But—"

"That's a brilliant idea, Ondine." Oscar cleared his throat. "I'm assuming you don't need any...*help*?"

"Nope," Ondine chirped in a too-bright voice. "I have it all under control. She—or he—will be back in the skies in no time."

"Great." Oscar stepped forward, tugging Emma along with him. "We'll leave you to it then. We have a date with Netflix."

But Emma kept frowning. Her gaze was focused on me. I could tell she didn't buy the story, even though Ondine had tried to play this whole thing off like it was no big deal. To help things out, I let out a small cry and twitched my wings.

"Oh dear." Oscar shook his head. "You better hurry, Ondine. It sounds like it's in pain."

"Yep! Gotta get going." Ondine swallowed hard and took off down the hallway before Oscar had a chance to drag Emma away from the scene. My mind reeled as we left them behind. Should I have transformed back into my fae form and spoken to her? Maybe I could have explained to her what I was doing, offered up some kind of deal to keep her silent.

But no. Oscar had this under control. They'd appeared to be on some kind of date, so she clearly liked him. Hopefully, he could convince her not to run straight to Nemain.

Ondine rushed to the back door with the kind of ferocity that suggested a killer clown was after her, not one of her fellow fae. When we reached the end of the long hallway, she gently sat me down on the floor and backed away.

"I'm assuming you're who I think you are and not just some random raven." She sucked in a breath, tears in her eyes. "I'm going to have to leave you here. Please be careful, and..." She dropped her voice to a whisper. "Please get Elise out of there."

I waited for a minute after she rushed away before transforming back into my fae form. When I'd first realised I could shift, it had been an excruciating, difficult process that left welts of pain all over my body. Now, I hardly even had to think about it.

Still, it took a lot out of me.

Sucking in deep lungfuls of air, I pushed up off my knees and cracked open the door. Moira was inside the Court within seconds, hastily handing me my clothes. I jumped into my jeans, shrugged my shirt over my head, and then we opened the door for the guys.

INNOCENT UNTIL PROVEN FAE

"How did it go?" Ronan asked in a low voice, carefully edging his body in front of mine as he peered down the quiet hallway.

"Fine. Mostly," I said.

Moira arched a brow. "Mostly?"

"We ran into Emma and Oscar." I pursed my lips. "He seemed cool with it, but Emma seemed a little shaken. I don't think it's anything to worry about though. He'll keep her busy long enough for us to get in and out."

"Right." Tiarnan gave a nod. "Where's the dungeons?"

I pointed, straight in the direction that would lead us back into the heart of the Court. "That way."

21

_J_ ake's invisibility would certainly come in handy right about now. After we'd slowly crept down the hallway, we came to a crossroads in the path. We needed to somehow edge our way past the lobby and then back through the left to go to the opposite wing in the building. Even though we'd done our best to time our little visit, some fae were night owls.

I poked out my head to see a Fianna guard stride back and forth in the glittering lobby. His gaze was alert as he glanced around him, but his body reflected that of someone totally at ease. He held his hands loosely behind his back. His shoulders were slumped a little forward. No tension. Nothing to suggest that he expected anyone to be dumb enough to infiltrate this place.

I waited until his back was turned our way, and then I motioned for the others to follow. With a deep breath, I scurried across the back wall of the lobby, dipping out of sight just in time.

Moira hissed as she slid in next to me. I glanced back at Tiarnan and Ronan. Neither of them had moved from their spot. I waved my arms, frantically trying to tell them to *come on.*

Ronan shook his head. "*Go,*" he mouthed.

"*What the hell are they doing?*" I mouthed to Moira.

She shrugged.

The guard's footsteps grew louder as we hunkered in the hallway. I took one last glance at Ronan. He waved his hands emphatically, motioning toward the approaching guard with growing alarm on his face.

With a sigh, I moved off down the hallway, keeping my back tight against the wall. We reached the door that led into the dungeons and slipped inside before the guard could spot us creeping around.

As soon as I shut it behind us, I risked a word aloud. "Why did they stay behind?"

Moira motioned at her feet. "You've heard Ronan, right? He's loud. I mean, you used to be pretty noisy yourself, but you've become super light on your feet lately."

"That doesn't explain Tiarnan," I said.

"The Fianna. It's one of their platitudes or whatever. They never leave a man behind."

I arched a brow. "We're talking about the same Tiarnan, right? The one who fled London because he couldn't face what he'd done against the Court?"

"And yet he's back." She shrugged. "It's either that or they're planning to trap us in these dungeons for Nemain."

A chill swept down my spine. "You don't think...?"

"Honestly, there's no telling who to trust these days," she said. "Any fae who isn't an enemy now can

INNOCENT UNTIL PROVEN FAE

be made an enemy, if Nemain decides that's how she wants to play things. She can make us do whatever she wants."

"Do you think I was wrong to bring Tiarnan here?"

She gave me a sad smile and squeezed my shoulder. "We can't stop doing things for fear of who she might be controlling. If we do, then she wins. Now, come on. Let's get our friend the hell out of here."

Moira took off down the winding stone stairs that had been smoothed over from centuries of use. My heart pounded hard as I followed after, her words ringing in my ears. She'd made a point that I wished I could shake out of my head, one that was far too likely for comfort.

Moira was right. Nemain could control any member of her Court with just a few small words. Often, there were loopholes in the commands of Princes and Princesses. I knew that all too well. But, if she were careful and thorough, she could twist someone enough to control their every movement.

Could that include Tiarnan to the point where she could change what I heard in his mind? It was a chilling thought, one that sent ice into the very depths of my bones. Shivering, I pressed down the stairs after Moira. If my suspicions were true, there was nothing I could do about it now. We were inside the Court. The only way out was back where we'd come from, right back into the arms of Tiarnan.

When we reached the bottom of the stairwell, I grabbed one of the burning torches from the wall, and Moira did the same. Quietly, we made our way through the winding, dark passages of the dungeons.

These old passageways were thin with low ceilings that threatened to knock us in the head. Once used for maintenance beneath the surface of the power station, they were now home to any number of spiders, cobwebs, and prisoners.

We reached a large room with cages set into the walls without encountering a single guard on the way. There was one lone prisoner in a tiny cell at the far end of the room.

"Clark! Moira!" Elise jumped to her feet, her silver hair knotted and frizzed. Her dark blue dress was stained brown, and her eyes, usually so bright and cheerful, were surrounded by purple bruises. My heart leapt into my throat, both at the relief of finding her here and at how ragged and tired she looked.

We rushed across the room and stood before her cell. Moira sunk down on her knees, fiddling with the deadbolt.

Elise's wide eyes searched my face. "I can't believe you're here. Does that mean Balor has taken back the Court?" She craned her neck to glance behind me at the tunnel that disappeared into darkness. "Is he back on the throne?"

"I'm afraid not," I said softly.

"Well then, where is he?" Elise's voice cracked on the last word.

She and Balor had known each other for decades. They'd had each other's backs for just as long. Secretly, she'd served as his second-in-command. They'd kept it under wraps to keep enemies on their toes. Elise was the bubbly, friendly, studious one who worked on intel with Kyle and didn't step foot out in the field. They'd correctly suspected that no one would assume she was

INNOCENT UNTIL PROVEN FAE

the one who could take over the Court if something happened to the Prince. Duncan or Cormac, too powerful warriors, had been more obvious choices.

Elise never really talked about it, but I knew she took a lot of pride in Balor's trust and respect in her. She thought he'd come to save her, the Prince she'd served so long. I wish I didn't have to tell her that he hadn't.

"He and Kyle are working on something else," I said with a strained smile. "An army, some more allies. We're not ready to invade just yet, so we've come to break you out of here now. We didn't want you to have to spend another night inside of this cage."

Her eyes widened even more as she flicked her gaze between me and Moira, who was making quick work of the lock. "Guys, you really shouldn't have done this. Nemain needs to be taken down, and it needs to happen now. That's way more important than getting me out of this damn cell."

"Yeah, well, there we're going to have to disagree," Moira said, smiling when the lock clicked open. "You are more important to us than a damn throne."

Elise nibbled her bottom lip before carefully pushing at the bars. "It's just that she is totally going to catch us. You know that, right?"

"Nah, we're good." Moira pulled the cage door open all the way. "We've got you."

"How do you know she isn't on her way here now?" Elise rubbed her palms against her shirt, both feet still firmly inside the cage. What had Nemain been doing to her? She was clearly too afraid to even leave her cell.

"We have two fantastic fighters on look-out duty,"

163

I said. "Even if she knows we're here, they'll stop her from getting to us."

Elise looked skeptical. "Two fighters? Who? I thought everyone but you two and Kyle were stuck inside the Court."

"Now isn't the time to go into details." Moira reached into the cell and hauled Elise out.

Just as her bare feet hit the stone floor, the world was consumed with the screaming sound of alarms. The room lit up with red, bright lights pulsing against the walls. We were in a disco of fear.

"Shit," Moira muttered, pulling her sword from the sheath around her waist. "We must have tripped some kind of alarm."

"That or Tiarnan turned us in," I said.

"*Tiarnan?*" Elise's voice went high-pitched as she stared at us with incredulous eyes. "You actually brought Tiarnan here to help me escape? The guy who wanted to turn us over to Fionn? Oh my god, we're doomed."

"We're not doomed," I said firmly. "We're going to get out of here. Alive."

The three of us rushed through the twisty passageways that led back to the stone stairs. Up and up we went, coming to a stop at the wooden door to exit the dungeons. Moira sucked in a deep breath and placed her ear against it, waiting with her eyes closed as she listened to the sounds in the hallways.

"There's a hell of a lot of pounding feet, and I'm pretty sure they're headed this way," she said, closing her eyes. "We're not getting out of this without a fight. Better out there than in here. We'll be forced back down the steps to where the cages are."

"Okay." I nodded. "You ready?"

"I'm not," Elise said in a weak voice.

Moira ignored her. She threw open the door and went storming out, sword raised high. We had only a moment to catch sight of what we faced. At least a dozen Fianna were rushing down the hallway toward us. Nemain strode quickly behind them, her face transfixed with a delighted smile. Her gaze zeroed in on me, and then she winked.

"Where the hell are Tiarnan and Ronan?" I shouted at Moira. They were nowhere to be seen. The hallway where they'd been waiting was now filled with Fianna, but there was no sign at all that there'd been a fight. My heart squeezed tight. Had they really betrayed us? Had they truly done the worst possible thing and turned us in?

Tears pricked the corners of my eyes. I was an idiot to have ever given them a second chance. I'd just so desperately wanted to believe them. All my life, I'd been alone. It's hard to make friends when you're on the run, constantly looking over your shoulder to make sure no one is following too close. I'd thought I liked it that way. I'd been wrong.

I wanted a Court. I wanted friends. I wanted ride or dies.

So much so that I'd been dumb enough to trust those who had once wronged me.

"Clark," Moira warned, her voice snapping me back into the present.

Sorrow still filled my gut as I watched the Fianna rush toward us. A few more steps, and they'd be within sword distance. The three of us would have to fight for our lives, and Elise didn't even have a pencil to stab into someone's throat.

With a deep breath, I closed my eyes and focused on the sorrow, calling for it, letting the pain of it all charge through me. And then I opened my mouth and screamed.

My voice echoed off the walls as the force of my magic tore through the corridor. It slammed hard into the Fianna, knocking every single one of them to the ground. Only Nemain was far enough back to evade the attack.

She slowed to a stop, her mouth agape. I stared at her. She stared at me. And then the three of us turned and got the hell out of dodge.

22

"Um, what the hell was that?" Elise asked when we were safely across the back lawn of the Court and into London's streets. "How long have you been able to knock out warrior fae just by shouting at them?"

"Hmm." I lifted a finger and cocked my head. "Approximately three days. Maybe a little longer if you count the time I accidentally knocked out some shifters."

"Damn good stuff." Moira grinned. "Even Nemain was shocked by it. Did you know that the Morrigan—"

A dark power whispered across my skin. Swallowing hard, I turned away from Moira, letting my eyes drift to where a shadowy form lurked in the alley just behind us. Balor stepped out from the depths of it, his single visible eye flashing with anger.

"Kyle tried to tell me that you wouldn't dare do something this stupid, but I can see that he was wrong and I was right." His voice was a low growl, and for once, his anger wasn't directed at me solely. "How could you break into the Crimson Court, alone, without even telling me? What in the name of the seven were you two bloody thinking?"

He curled his hands into fists and stalked toward us, but his expression softened when he spotted Elise hiding just behind me. His eyebrows lifted, the corners of his lips tilted up. "Elise? You're okay."

"I am okay." Her voice was soft. "Because Moira and Clark risked their lives to save me."

He furrowed his brows, sighed. "I'm sorry I didn't come for you myself. Instead of charging in without a plan, I've been trying to build up an unstoppable force to remove Nemain from the throne. As long as she's still living, you are bound to her. She could order you to walk right back through that door if she wanted to."

Balor glanced around. "Where are those two males who insist on following you around everywhere you go?"

"Seems they may have been the reason we almost got caught."

Balor's expression darkened. "Tell me everything."

And so, we filled him in.

~

*M*oira and Elise started back toward the flat while Balor and I took a moment to chat. It didn't take long before the horrible dark magic had returned to our feet, brought on by nothing more than the thrill I felt when Balor looked at me.

"There's something wrong with this," I said, tears

INNOCENT UNTIL PROVEN FAE

flooding into my eyes. I glanced around at the dark cloud pulsing all around us. "This isn't normal. It isn't right. Honestly, Balor. It terrifies me. You saw what happened to Kyle. He could have been hurt far worse than he was..."

I didn't speak the next words aloud, but I couldn't help but think them: our love could kill someone.

"There's something I need to tell you," Balor said in a strained voice. He took a step closer to me, and the cloud pulsed. Sucking in a deep breath, he closed his eyes. "Kyle told me what you asked of him."

My heart lurched. "You mean, the bit where I asked him to research this magic."

"You asked him to look into it, specifically to find out if there was anything wrong."

I closed my eyes and sighed. "I did. Please don't get angry, Balor. But—"

"He looked into it. And he found an answer."

Chills swept along my skin. There was something about the tone of his voice that only ramped my fear up another notch. I flipped my eyes back open, only to find that the terrible cloud of dark magic had vanished into the night.

"What's happening between us...it's not the mating bond, is it?" I asked in a small, still voice.

He gave a quick shake of his head, and all the hope and happiness I'd begun to feel deflated from my body within an instant.

Balor and I hadn't truly mated. Whatever had happened between us was something else. Something dark and terrible. Something that we would have to end. Perhaps it had happened because of the

169

JENNA WOLFHART

prophecy. The supernatural world trying to right a wrong.

And that wrong thing was us.

"The mating bond isn't what is causing these issues between us, Clark," he said quietly, "though we *have* mated, we have bonded. It's just much, much more complicated than that. Much more complicated than I could have ever dreamed."

I took a slow step closer to him. "If it isn't the mating bond, then what is it?"

"You need to open your eyes and remember. You need to accept who you are." A beat passed. "And I do, too."

I stared up at him, my heart twisting like a snake. "You don't have to accept it, Balor, because I'm *not* the Morrigan."

"Search for the truth deep down inside of you, Clark. You know it's there, even if you try to push it aside." He crossed the distance between us then, and sparks bounced from his body to mine. I shook my head as I watched the dark smokey tendrils of magic wrap around us.

I swallowed hard. "Fine. Let's pretend for a minute that you're right. What would our screwed up bond have to do with me being the Morrigan?"

"Since you spent most of your life on the run, I assume you haven't read the full tales of the Morrigan," he said quietly.

"No, but I know the highlights," I said.

"The Morrigan," he said, taking a deep breath before continuing, "has always had a tumultuous relationship with the smiter."

170

INNOCENT UNTIL PROVEN FAE

All the blood drained from my face. "The smiter. You mean...you?"

Oh my god, had Balor been alive that long? Had he wed different versions of the same female, over and over again? Had they mated? Is that why our own bond had gone wrong? He was trying to rewrite his bond with someone else.

"Clark." Balor took my hand in his and pressed it to his heart. I could feel the rhythmic beating, felt the life and magic pour from his body and into mine. Out of the corner of my eye, I saw the cloud forming once again. Sparks of dangerous energy whorled around us, biting at my skin. "There have been many smiters across the centuries. None of the books mention reincarnation, so I never thought much of it. But there are two souls that seem to live on in this world. The Morrigan, and...and me."

I blinked up at him and took a step back. "You're trying to tell me that you're the reincarnation of some other Balor?"

He gave an almost imperceptible nod. "Another smiter, yes. I've been having dreams, too, of a time long since past. Far before I was born. And, by my side, was you."

"That's impossible." I ripped my hand out of his and shook my head. This was too much. I wasn't some long forgotten Queen, and I certainly wasn't forged in space and time with someone else, not even Balor. I'd grown up in a world where magic reigned supreme, but this was far too much for me to swallow.

"It's the truth."

"Then, why the dark magic?" I asked, eyes wide. "If

we're some kind of fated reincarnated mates, then our bond shouldn't be so volatile. It should feel right. It shouldn't be dangerous to everyone who comes near us."

"Because we haven't always been mates." He sighed, dragged a hand down his face. "Kyle did some research. You and I...it's a toss of a coin. We either love each other or hate each other, and it can never be in between. And until the magic decides what we are..."

"It will try to bring us together and rip us apart at the same damn time," I whispered.

Balor pursed his lips, and then nodded. "So, you believe me."

I let out a ragged sigh. "No. Yes. I don't know. Maybe. This whole thing is a little overwhelming, I'm not going to lie."

"You know you're the Morrigan, right?"

I squeezed my eyes tight. "But how, Balor? The Morrigan is the most powerful fae alive. I'm part shifter. I'm not even full fae. And my powers...well, they're a joke."

"Are they?" He sounded closer now, so close that I could reach out and touch him, but I was scared to make contact. As long as that magical storm threatened to consume us, we needed to keep some distance.

"Yes. I'm slower than you. I'm not that strong of a fighter."

"In the span of a few months, you've gone from not being able to fight at all to taking down dozens of enemies at once. You can transform into a raven and call them to your aide. And when you shout, even the strongest fighters fall." He wrapped a tendril of hair around his finger and pushed it behind my ear. "I can't even begin to imagine how powerful you'll be in another few months."

"This is a lot to process," I whispered to him.

"I know." He gave me a sad smile. "It's a lot for me to process, too. The smiter hasn't always used his powers for good. He—*I* have let my rage and anger control me. I've done some terrible things in my past lives."

"You might share souls, and you might be some version of him." I reached up and placed my palm on his cheek. "But you are not any of these past selves, Balor. You're you and only you. This doesn't change who you are."

"No, Clark. I'm afraid I can't agree. This changes everything." Slowly, Balor knelt to the ground before me and bowed his head, dark silver-streaked hair hanging into his eyes. "My Queen."

23

"No more of this Queen business," I hissed at Balor as we caught up to Elise and Moira on the trek back to the flat. My heartbeat was loud in my ears as I replayed the moment Balor knelt before me. In all our many moments spent together, I'd learned a lot about the former Prince. He was strong, powerful, ferocious, and quick to anger. And he had pride. He would never kneel before a single soul, especially one who wore no crown.

That whole moment outside of the Court felt like a distant dream.

A dream I'd had before. Moments from our past lives had begun to flood back into my mind. Thrones and knights, battles and swords. Beds beneath canopies, strolls through thick forests. Ships sailing deep into the night.

It was all there in the back of my mind, threatening to break free of whatever spell had kept it locked in there all these years.

The realisation of the truth was washing over me.

I'd tried so hard to push it away, but there was no stopping it now.

I was the Morrigan.

Wow. It was tough to even think the words, much less say them aloud.

I am the Morrigan.

The dreams, the powers, the ravens. It had all been there, taunting me for months. It still didn't explain why or how, but those were questions I might never find the answer to.

~

*B*ack in the flat, we found Kyle had managed to clean up most of the mess. He'd already gotten three computers lined up on the floor. He sat cross-legged before them, munching on some take-away pizza from the shop next door.

"Oh, hi," he said around a mouthful of food. "Where've you guys been?"

Elise slid into the flat just behind us, and a slice of pizza slipped from Kyle's hand to fall flat on the floor. Marinara sauce splattered on one of the new monitors, painting it red.

"Holy shit." Kyle jumped to his feet and grinned. "You're alive. You're out. Is Ondine with you?"

Poor guy. I didn't have the heart to tell him that Ondine opted to stay at the Court, the orders of her Queen preventing her from doing anything else. "We didn't have time to find her."

"Ah." His smile dimmed. "That's alright. Just glad to see Elise made it out of there."

INNOCENT UNTIL PROVEN FAE

I gave Kyle a sad smile. "We'll get Ondine out next. I swear. We just need a good plan."

"Unfortunately, none of our plans have worked so far," Balor said as he took a seat on the floor to join our circle. He looked out of place like this, a Prince without a throne. "Maeve has gone missing. We need to find her and the rest of the Sluagh, more for London's sake than anything else. But we have no way of knowing how long it will take to track her down."

"Meanwhile, Jake's phone appears to be dead." Kyle leaned back, typed a few keys, and shook his head. "The number has been completely disconnected."

"And we'd need him and his spell book to change Maeve and the other Sluagh back into fae," Moira said, explaining things to Elise.

"This is a disaster," Elise said. "What about the vampires? Clark, you said that Matteo has warmed up to you?"

"I really wouldn't call it warm," I said. "He's still Matteo, if you know what I mean. And he's not going to fight now when he wouldn't fight before. Things are working well for him at the moment."

"We might have been able to use Ronan to get the Pack to return, but..." Balor trailed off.

"He completely sold us out," Moira filled in. "Him and that arsehole, Tiarnan."

"Maybe the five of us should just go for it?" I asked, my voice getting more and more high-pitched with every word. "If I get close enough to Nemain, I could use my, erm, Morrigan power, erm, to knock her out."

God, I hated saying it out loud.

JENNA WOLFHART

"So, you're finally copping onto the fact that you're the Morrigan," Moira said dryly.

"It's about damn time," Elise added.

Kyle quirked a grin. "Damn straight."

"Honestly, if you start making a big deal out of it, I'll throw the Morrigan's power at *you*." I crossed my arms and glared at each of them in turn.

"I have an idea," Kyle said suddenly. "Nemain plans to go to the Ivory Court and convince them to join her in an alliance, right?"

We all nodded.

"You just saw her. She's still in London. What if we go now and beat her to it? After they hear what she's done, they might just join us instead. That way, we don't have to keep chasing sorcerers, Sluagh, and vampires all over a city full of humans who hate us."

I arched a brow, glanced at Balor. It wasn't a terrible idea.

"Go to the Ivory Court," Balor said with a slow nod. "It may be a risk travelling there. Nemain could have her Fianna on flight checking duty. But it's not a bad idea. Not a bad idea at all. Clark, what do you think?"

Four sets of eyes turned to me. I blinked and swallowed hard, caught off guard by the intensity of their gazes. "It sounds like it might be the only plan we have. So, if you decide we should go, then I won't argue."

"I'm not the one making the decision. You are."

"Oh, come on." I let out a strangled laugh and glanced to Moira, whose gaze was as serious as Balor's. "The Prince of the Crimson Court should decide how we're going to——"

"You're our Queen." Moira bowed her head and placed her sword on the ground before me. "Give your orders."

Blood rushed into my cheeks as I stared at my friend, the last person in the world I wanted bowing down to me. I wasn't a ruler, regardless of whether or not the Morrigan's soul resided within my own. I didn't know anything about commanding an army, let alone a whole kingdom.

Still, I cleared my throat and stood. "Okay, if you want an order, I'll give you orders. We're going to pay a visit to the Ivory Court."

24

The Ivory Court was one of seven. Centuries ago, most fae lived on a small section of the globe, choosing to keep among themselves. Over time, the Courts had begun to spread out, flowing with the human continents. The Crimson Court had settled in London, covering most of Europe. The Ivory Court was in Africa.

Balor leaned close to Kyle's screen as our resident computer expert typed away with his tongue stuck out between his teeth. "Think you can make it so we don't have to use our real names?"

"We'd need some fake passports for that," Kyle said in a huff. "I could probably rustle some up, but it will take a few days."

Elise paced from one end of the room to another, her face pinched tight. "Nemain will somehow figure out what we're up to. She'll set a trap."

"Even Nemain isn't all-knowing," I said with a frown. "Right now, she thinks we're running like

JENNA WOLFHART

lunatics around London. She's not going to expect us to jet off and leave the city in her hands."

Elise nibbled on her bottom lip. "She thinks two steps ahead of the rest of us. I think it's her power. She can anticipate other people's moves. Have you ever seen her surprised? Caught off guard? It's because she's visualising everything."

"Yeah, I saw her caught off guard," I said. "Tonight when I used my Morrigan power against her."

"She didn't anticipate that because she didn't know what you are." Elise sucked in a deep lungful of air. "She won't make the same mistake twice. Nemain has spent a lot of time with the Morrigan. She'll know what your power means. Hell, she's probably already planning some kind of retaliation against you as we speak."

I knew all about Nemain and her history with the Morrigan. She'd plotted against her for years, desperate to rise up the ranks and take her crown. It had worked, for a little while at least. But karma would come bite her on the ass. Because the Morrigan? She now knew exactly what Nemain was capable of.

"What would you have us do instead?" I asked her.

"I don't know," she said, eyes filling with tears as she shook her head. "Nemain has been messing with my mind, and I no longer know what thought is mine and what isn't. You probably shouldn't listen to me. Who knows if I'm saying something she wants me to say."

I sighed, crossed the room, and wrapped my arms around her just as the tears began to slide down her cheeks. Squeezing tight, I held her against my chest, letting the pain and fear eke out of her eyes and into my shirt.

"I'm so sorry, Clark. I'm a mess."

"Don't apologise. It's not your fault. As soon as we have her off that throne, you won't have to worry about her anymore."

"Clark," Balor said, his voice a warning.

I glanced over the top of Elise's head. He stood still in the center of the room, his entire body taut with tension. He cocked his head, listening. To my still untrained ears, nothing was amiss.

Moira frowned. Even Kyle's back snapped tight.

"What the hell?" Kyle murmured. He punched a few keys on the keyboard, and a crackling video came into view. Dozens of humans were crowded on the sidewalk outside of the building. Some were carrying steel bats. Others had knives. They were chanting something, their arms pounding the air in unison. Suddenly, I felt sick.

"Okay, *now* Nemain has found us," I said in a whisper, staring at the screen where dozens more humans suddenly joined the mob. "And she's sent the humans to do her dirty work for her."

"What the hell do we do?" Moira asked. "We can't just go out there and start slicing through humans."

"No, and Nemain would be counting on that," I murmured.

Narrowing my eyes, I strode closer to the screen and peered down at the video. Elise had been right. Nemain had decided to set a trap, but instead of waiting until we were on the flight, she'd done it here.

"Tiarnan must have told her where we are." I

scowled. "I can't believe he managed to fool me again."

"She'd probably already gotten to him first," Elise said. "That's how she works. She sneaks in when you aren't expecting it."

"Ah, hi." Henry bobbed his head in the doorway and glanced around. "Glad to see you've spruced the place up after the, ah, unfortunate incident. You manage to track down those youths?"

"Yeah. Thanks for the help, Henry."

"Oh, good," he said with a smile. "Because when I started to think things over again, I realised I was mixing up the youths with a different lot. The ones who stole your computers didn't go into the corner shop."

"No worries. We tracked them down."

He glanced at the computer screen we were all huddled around, and winced. "So, I guess you've seen what's happening out there. Hate to see that it's come to this. I honestly thought we humans could be more understanding and accepting of all you supernaturals, but maybe we just aren't there yet."

"Yeah, I'd say not," Moira said. "They're two seconds away from ripping off the front door and storming in here. How many humans you got in the building?"

"Quite a few, some with children." Henry pursed his lips. "And they'll all be home. It is the middle of the night, after all."

"Maybe we should just go out there and give ourselves up to them," I said.

In unison, the entire room shouted, "NO!" Including Henry.

"Wow, you guys need to calm down," I said, holding up my hands. "Just think about it. They're out there demanding our heads. There are tons of innocent humans in here. If the mob gets too riled up, they'll swarm, and then someone will end up hurt."

"You're not going out there, love," Henry said with a sad smile. "If you do, they'll probably kill you. No, the police are on their way. I just don't think you should be here when they arrive. They're arresting all kinds of supes right now just for being alive. I'll get you out the back way."

One day, I would have to find a way to repay this little man for everything he'd done to help me.

We went out through Henry's homey flat, scaled down the fire escape, and then took off through the back alleys of East London. We'd spent so much time running these past few weeks, I was aching for a fight. But not like this, and not with humans. Nemain needed to be stopped.

We huddled in the doorway of an abandoned storefront after putting several blocks between us and the mob. The London chill had descended upon the night, and I blew against my hands to keep them warm. None of us had grabbed coats. There hadn't been the time.

"You manage to get our flights booked?" I asked Kyle.

"Yeah, but it's not leaving until tomorrow night. It was the earliest one I could get. All the others were booked."

"Great," Moira said. "We'll have to camp out on the streets for the rest of the night."

"We could use our time more wisely than that,"

JENNA WOLFHART

Kyle said with a shrug. "You said you got in and out through a back door, right? There weren't security cameras then, but Nemain won't make the same mistake twice. We could stake things out. See how they improve their systems. Watch. Then, when we finally do attack, we'll have all the information we need."

Great. More surveillance. Exactly what I wanted to do after a long, crazy night.

"I vote bed, and then a hot bath. We could book a hotel room and crash for a few hours, forget who we are and why we have to fight so hard just to exist."

Elise bowed her head, followed by Kyle. "As you wish, my Queen."

I stared at them all, and then laughed. "Guys, I was just kidding. It was a joke. Has my magic done something to you or something? Please tell me it's not like the Princely bond."

"The Morrigan has never had a magical bond with her subjects," Balor said. "She doesn't need one. We willingly serve."

"Okay, stop with this shite." I held up my hands and stepped back. "It feels awkward to hear you calling me your Queen. I'm just Clark."

"You need to get used to hearing it from us. Soon, every fae in the world will be calling you that." Elise smiled. "As the Morrigan, you are our Queen."

"Yep, so it's your call, Highness," Moira quirked. "Hotel or stalking duty. What'll it be?"

"Come on," I said with a sigh. "Let's go lurk around in some bushes."

25

Things were not any better back at the Crimson Court. Understatement of the year, actually. We'd thought that a mob of humans had surrounded the flat's building, but that had been nothing compared to the amount of human bodies crushing the Great Lawn at Court. The stretch of green that separated the old power station from the river was usually empty, save the occasional random tourist too nosy for her own good.

Now, it was crammed tight full of chanting, roaring humans. Some had signs they were waving in the air. The back of them faced us, so we couldn't see what they said. But I was pretty sure we had a damn good idea.

Whatever Nemain had said to the humans to get them to come after us had backfired. And now they were coming for her, too.

"I'd say something about karma, but I'm worried about everyone inside," Moira said.

Balor crossed his arms over his chest and frowned,

JENNA WOLFHART

those pinched lines appearing on his forehead. "We need to de-escalate the situation before things get out of control. One side will eventually fire the first shot. You know what will happen then."

All it would take was one person—fae or human—to kick off the kind of fight that would only end in rivers of blood.

"Boss?" Kyle twisted toward me, his face as white as the clouds blowing over our heads. He wasn't exactly used to field work, and he was about to get a crash course in it.

Honestly, I wished they'd stop with the boss stuff, but now was not the time to throw responsibility off my shoulders like an old, too-warm coat. Lives were at stake here. Not only humans but fae who were stuck inside. They'd had no say in being here. They were a slave to their bond. If this place went up in flames, they probably wouldn't even have free will enough to run.

"There's no talking the humans down at this point," I said quietly. "Not unless someone they respected came to them and made some sort of announcement."

"Like who?" Balor frowned.

"The Mayor," Kyle said. "He's the one who has been making all these anti-supernatural laws. It's clearly given them an incentive to come after us. If he would tell them to stand down, I bet they would."

"Great idea," Moira said dryly. "But how the hell are we going to get that arsehole to stand up for protecting fae? He's the very reason all of this is happening in the first place."

"Politics," I said quickly. "We need to offer him something he can't refuse."

Elise let out a nervous giggle. "Guys, we never should have started calling her Queen. She's already starting to sound like the Godfather."

"I like it," Balor said, pride flickering in his orange eye. "You're thinking like a leader now, not just a fighter."

"And what exactly are we going to offer Head Arsehole?" Moira asked. "From what I can see, we don't have much."

I cleared my throat. "I mean, I have an idea, but you're probably not going to like it."

"I really don't like it when you say that," Balor said.

"Well, you know how Matteo agreed to turn Jake into a vampire if—"

"No." Balor closed his eyes and pinched the bridge of his nose. "Clark, no."

"Since Jake has disappeared into the ether, I feel like we might be able to make a substitution. It might take a little negotiation, but I have a feeling Matteo wouldn't mind being the sire of the Mayor of London."

"This is a terrible idea."

"And after he goes through the change, he might have different views on his laws..." Moira trailed off. "My god, Clark. That's bloody brilliant."

"Why, thank you." I gave a curtsy, even though I was wearing jeans. "Now, any idea how we get an audience with the Mayor?"

Something in the corner of my eye caught my attention. It was a flash of burning red through the crowd on the far left of the building. Frowning, I stared and waited for it to return. Were the fae about to launch an attack on the humans?

We might not have the time to call the Mayor, after all.

"Kyle," I said, turning his way. "I need you to do your thing and get us in touch with the Mayor. Elise, keep him company and an eye out. You know how to fight. He doesn't. Stick together." I turned to Moira next. "I have a bad feeling the fae are about to attack. There's not enough time for us to check out the whole place together. You go right. Balor, take the back. And I'll check out the left."

Balor's smile was soft as he gave me a nod. "And what would you like us to do if we encounter some fae readying themselves for attack?"

"Disarm them. Knock them out. Do whatever you have to do in order to stop them." I paused just as I started to walk away. "Try not to kill them. They're not of their own minds."

The three of us split up while Kyle got on the phone to the Mayor. We edged around the chanting crowd, disappearing into the shadowy tree line that stood to attention around the boundary of the property. The red flash had come from the left side of the building, which was why I'd chosen it myself. My powers were getting stronger. If Nemain was out here, I wanted to take her on myself.

I sneaked into the midst of the trees, breathing in the fresh scent of pine mixed with the smog of the city. The lights that edged the roof lit up the stretch of lawn that reached out toward me. The crowd had thinned into nothing back here. The humans were too

INNOCENT UNTIL PROVEN FAE

focused on the front steps to worry about what was going on in the back.

With a deep breath, I stole across the lawn.

"Hi, Clark." Nemain's smile was bright as she stepped out of the shadows. "What a strange coincidence to find you here."

"It's not a coincidence at all, and you know it." I glanced around us, expecting her team of warriors to come rushing in at any moment, but she merely continued to stand alone before me with that eerie smile plastered across her face. "You know, if you're not careful, you're going to lose this Court and that throne. The humans are out for blood."

"Yes, I've noticed," she said sweetly. "The thing is, we're far stronger and far faster. Plus, we have healers who can fix any wound. All we have to do is target the frontlines, and that mob out there will fall within seconds."

My heart squeezed tight. "You're honestly going to kill a hundred innocents, just to keep your throne."

"They don't look like innocents to me. They look like a vicious, angry mob that must be put down, like a rabid wolf."

I crossed my arms and stood tall. "I can't allow you to do that."

"Oh yeah?" She laughed. "And what do you think you're going to do about it?"

With a deep breath, I curled my hands into fists and focused on the pain and anger inside of me. Just one scream, and she'd be down for the count. I didn't know how long it would keep her unconscious, but I had to hope it would be long enough to wrestle control over the Court. She wouldn't be able to control a

JENNA WOLFHART

damn thing if her mind wasn't awake, dealing magic out like pills.

I opened my mouth to scream, but something white, hot, and electric slammed into me before the scream ripped from my throat.

The world tipped sideways beneath me. My nose slammed hard into the dirt.

~

"Wake up, wake up," a sweet voice whispered into my ear. I cracked open my eyes, my head split in two from the pounding against my skull. My face was smashed against a cold, stone ground, and my legs were twisted beneath me. With a groan, I pushed up to get my bearings.

I was no longer on the Great Lawn outside of Court. Instead, I found myself in a dark room lit only by two torches on the thick stone walls. Darkness and dust swirled all around me, closing in tight like a blanket of death.

Nemain squatted outside the cage bars, grinning in at me. "There she is. Took you awhile to wake up. That spell did you dirty."

I narrowed my eyes and clutched the dirt, fingernails scraping the stone. "What the hell did you do to me?"

"Who me?" She laughed and placed a hand against her heart, fluttering her eyelashes. "Absolutely nothing. The pain you're feeling most likely came from her."

Another form stepped out of the shadows. When the orange light flickered across her face, I stiffened.

192

INNOCENT UNTIL PROVEN FAE

Elena stood before me, her red cloak draped around her shoulders, a painted smile curling up to meet her eyes. "Hi, there. Remember me?"

I jumped to my feet, fists shaking. "You."

"Yes, me." She cocked an eyebrow. "You really thought that we were done? Jake should have told you that I never let go of a prize once I've set my eyes on it."

I whirled toward Nemain. "I thought you were smart, but I was wrong. Teaming up with this sorcerer is the worst decision you've made yet. She wants to consume fae souls so that she can become one of us."

"I know all about her little plan." Nemain chuckled and took a step away from the cage. "She came to me after you and your little friends stalked her at her club. Did you know it is illegal now for a supernatural to go wandering the city at night? Not only that, but you scared an innocent. The sentence for your actions is death."

"I get his soul though." Elena jerked her thumb toward a cage at the far end of the room. The light from the torches didn't reach that far, so all I saw was a huddled form between the thick bars. "Your Queen here is taking yours."

Nemain hissed in response as my heart roared in my ears.

"What the hell are you talking about?" I asked.

"You shouldn't have said anything," Nemain said, her eyes flashing as she rounded on the girl. Her hands twitched by her side, the rage that lived deep within her desperate to get out. For a moment, I thought she might kill the sorcerer right then and there, but she finally let out a slow exhale and turned her attention back onto me. "I guess it's out, and I can't take it back now. Elena's spell can transfer your power to me. The thing is, I thought the Morrigan was gone from our world forever. When I saw what you could do, you have no idea what kind of gift that was to me. Now, I can take your power and become the Morrigan myself. I've never wanted anything more, Clark."

A shiver went through me. Nemain had spoken many lies in the days that I'd known her, going all the way back to when I'd been a child. But this right here...it was the biggest truth she'd ever uttered. A cold, harsh truth that slapped me in the face.

For centuries, Nemain had wanted one thing and one thing only: to become the most powerful fae alive. The Morrigan.

And now she was finally going to do it.

26

My execution was to be shortly after first light. She wanted to wait until the rest of the Court awakened to call a meeting in the throne room. There, she would sentence me to death and take my soul.

All before I could have a damn cup of coffee.

"I'd hoped she wouldn't get to you," a muffled voice spoke from the cell in the far end of the room. A familiar, deep voice that made my ears prick up.

"Who's there?" I asked, words echoing off the stone.

He shifted closer to the bars, but the shadows still obscured his face. "Tiarnan. Her Fianna caught me and Ronan while you were down here looking for Elise. When the alarms went off...sorry we weren't strong enough to fight them all off."

"Wait." I sat up straight. "You got caught? You didn't turn on us?"

He sighed. "I can see why it might seem that way.

But no, I didn't turn on you. That sorcerer is the one who has been feeding Nemain information."

My heart thumped hard. "And where the hell is Ronan?"

"He's in another one of these rooms. They had us in here together, but decided to separate us when we kept scheming ways to get out."

Relief shook through me. Of course, it was only short-lived. Sure, Tiarnan and Ronan hadn't betrayed us, again, but that didn't change the fact that we were all stuck in this dungeon with only hours left before our deaths.

"You didn't happen to come up with any good plans before he got moved, did you?" It was too much to hope for, I knew.

"Negative," he said. "Ronan tried shifting and using his brute strength, but these bars don't bend at all."

A beat passed in silence before he spoke again.

"What about your bird form? Would it be small enough to squeeze through those gaps?"

"There will be a spell," I replied. "Nemain is too smart for that trick."

"Then, no. I've got absolutely nothing."

With a heavy sigh, I laid back on the floor to stare up at the criss-crossing bars over my head. My entire body ached from the tense stress of the last few days. It felt as if my whole being had been run through a blender, one that had taken care to punch me in the eyes a few times. The last thing I wanted right now was sleep. But tiredness snatched at my face. It was a tunnel pulling me in, soft arms dragging me deep within the darkness of dreams.

n my chambers, I mulled over my unease. Nemain's actions had been giving me far more cause for alarm than before. At first, I had appreciated her desire to improve her lot in life. She was ambitious. Ambition could be admirable.

But it could also be full of darkness when taken too far.

Such as now.

Lady Edith had shown up dead the night before. A small wound from a tiny blade, straight into the heart. It was the attack of someone who knew what they were doing. Someone who had trained for this.

It had come shortly after my decision to end the war.

And now Nemain was on her way to see me.

A knock sounded on my door and I pressed my sweaty palms against my dress. There was no telling what Nemain might do in order to take her place higher in Court. Would she attempt to kill me outright? I found it hard to believe, unless her ambition had clouded her mind with vicious shades of red.

When I opened the door, Lady Nemain stood before me, her expression downturned as if she were in the middle of some deep, serious thoughts.

"Come on in, Nemain." I gestured her into my chambers and shut the door quietly behind me. "I hear you have some concerns."

"My Queen." She took a deep breath, and then gave me a timid smile. "I know I am only just a Lady, but I served as a Knight for you for years. I understand war."

"I would not argue with that."

"We cannot quit fighting. Not yet. Not when the prize is so close."

"And what prize are you referring to?" I arched a brow.

JENNA WOLFHART

"The throne, of course. You wish to rule the Courts as one, do you not?"

I pressed my lips firmly together. "I wish for peace within Faerie. Until now, there has been far too much strife, far too much bickering amongst ourselves. My fight was to end the fight. It is over now. All Courts save one have either surrendered or joined the alliance, and the last wishes to retain its independence. It is over."

Nemain's eyes flashed. My answer had not satisfied her. Not in the least.

"This is your mistake," she said. "They will kill you."

"That is enough," I said, clipping my words. "I have made my decision, and yet I have still allowed you to have your say. You may go now."

Her eyes flashed, but she turned to go. She would not make her move now, but I knew it would not be long before the snake lashed out. Would I see the strike before her fangs sank deep into my skin?

"The last you was better," she said as she cracked open the door. "The force of you and the smiter together is enough to burn down the whole world. Alone, you're both too hard and too soft. But you don't know what I'm talking about, do you? You never remember. So much untapped potential. When I'm finally you, I won't waste it."

2 7

My shirt was drenched in sweat when I finally awoke, images of my claustrophobic dreams clawing at my mind. I blinked hard and tried to get my vision to focus on what was before me: dirty stone ground, flickering torches, thick bars that buzzed with magic.

"That must have been one hell of a dream," Tiarnan murmured.

I jerked up my head. "What makes you say that?"

"You were chattering away," he said with a low chuckle. "Something about Nemain. You can't even escape her in your own damn dreams."

"It wasn't a dream. It was a vision. Of the past. A memory, really."

Something about the dream was nibbling on my brain. Something that Nemain had said. Obviously, she'd been an outright bitch to the Morrigan. To me. I needed to start thinking about myself as the same person I'd been back then. Because Nemain had made it more than clear that the memories were important.

The Morrigan never remembered her past selves. She never embraced who she'd once been.

Suddenly, I sprang to my feet. My entire body went hot as excitement flooded through me like a tidal wave.

"Holy shit," I said, eyes wide as I clung onto the bars. "All this time I thought Caer was talking about what I did, not who I've been. But I was wrong. It was there right in front of me this whole damn time."

Tiarnan had climbed to his feet, too. "Clark, I have no bloody idea what in the name of sanity you're talking about, but I'm glad it has you so hopeful all of a sudden. Mind filling me in on what's making you dance around your cage like a child with too much sugar?"

"That prophecy that Caer gave me. Remember it?" Tiarnan had been with me when we'd visited the Lake of the Dragon Mouth. He'd listened in on Balor's prophecy and tried to help me make sense of what we'd heard. But we'd *really* both slept on what she'd told me about myself.

"Oh yeah. How did it go again? Something about accepting what you did in the past to better enjoy the future?"

"No." My voice rose with excitement. "Her exact words were, 'The first step toward surviving the future is accepting the past.'"

Tiarnan gave a nod. "That was it. And she was right, wasn't she? You came clean to Balor, and he forgave you."

"That wasn't what Caer was talking about, Tiarnan. She was talking about my *past* past. As the Morrigan."

INNOCENT UNTIL PROVEN FAE

The dungeons went so silent that I swore I heard a pin drop onto the floor. Tiarnan let out a low whistle. "That makes a lot of sense. I see why you're excited now. She was talking about this moment right here, us stuck inside these cages, hours away from being sacrificed in some kind of dark magic spell."

"I have never been more certain of anything in my life."

He nodded. "So, what does that mean? How do you do that in a way that will get us out of here alive?"

I sucked in a long, sharp breath. "The Morrigan is inside of me, Tiarnan. She's a part of me, in all of her many forms, which means...her voices are deep within my soul. I need to push aside all of the boundaries I've erected around my mind so that I can hear her, so that we can all become one."

Another low whistle, this time with added concern flickering across his face. "I thought you put up those boundaries because hearing everyone's thoughts is far too much for you to handle without passing out."

"Yep." I pressed my sweaty hands against my jeans. "But I'm just going to have to do it, Tiarnan. If I don't, we won't live to see tomorrow."

28

*I*mages and thoughts flooded my head. Some were a part of memories I'd already dreamed, some were of a different Morrigan's life completely. Nemain was there, front and center, big flashing lights of warning going off in a chorus of a dozen shouts.

I fell to my knees, my entire body shaking as each voice rose louder, each scream trying to topple the last. They all wanted me to hear them, their whole story, their life from beginning to end.

Suddenly, it all went silent.

A door opened and closed in the distance, and footsteps echoed on the stone ground. Slowly, I pushed myself onto my feet and stood waiting for Nemain.

Make her talk. She likes to talk.

I wet my lips as Nemain strode into the room with her shoulders thrown back. She'd donned an all-black ensemble, and her makeup highlighted her sharp cheekbones and piercing eyes. She came to stand before me, dangling the keys.

"You know what this means, don't you?" she asked.

"No. Why don't you tell me?"

"It's time for you to lose your soul," she said with a laugh. "Which means the Morrigan will die. Again."

Stab her in the eyeball.

I bit back a smile. "Why don't you have any guards with you? Surely you don't think you can handle me all by yourself."

"You won't do anything. If you do, Tiarnan dies." She flicked her fingers at my fellow fae. He was pressed up against the bars, watching and listening. When she turned back to me, she stabbed the key into the lock and began to twist.

"I just have one more question."

She paused, eyebrow raised.

"What makes you think this sorcerer isn't going to want more?" I asked. "Once she turns herself into a fae, she's going to tell all her friends about it. They'll want a slice of the immortality pie, too. You know they'll be back."

Nemain let out a laugh. "Sometimes, I forget just how human you can act. Yes, I know she will be back. What's it to me? There will always be enemies, prisoners we can sacrifice. She will be doing me a favour by getting rid of the trash."

A shriek echoed in my skull, so loud it made me wince.

Nemain noticed, and her eyes became slits. "What was that?"

"I've had zero sleep in over twenty four hours, you haven't brought us water, and I'm going into caffeine withdrawal. I have a headache. That a problem?"

"Why the Morrigan would choose a half-fae is beyond me." She turned the lock and pulled open the door.

Heartbeat hammering, I stepped outside. The Morrigan voices inside of me had gone suspiciously quiet, which was about as helpful as the mind-numbing shriek had been. Where the hell had they gone right when I'd needed them most? Nemain was about to take me up the stairs to my death. If we were going to do something, it needed to be now.

Nemain grabbed my arm and dug her nails into my skin. "Come on then. Let's get this show on the road."

"Wait!" I shouted the words so loud they boomed all around us.

Nemain let out a huff of irritation. "Stop stalling. I'm getting impatient. You have no idea how long I have waited for this moment, and I'll not wait a moment more."

"I don't want to be the Morrigan," I said quickly, pulling something straight out of my ass.

"Okay." She twisted toward me, face scrunched up in confusion. But I could tell I'd gotten her attention by the flicker in her eye. "I don't see how that is at all relevant. As soon as we go up those stairs, you're done."

"There's something wrong with...this." I gestured up and down myself. "The whole Morrigan thing didn't take right with me. I think it might have something to do with the smiter."

I honestly had no idea what the hell I was rambling on about, but I was going to continue to go with it. At the very least, it was stalling Nemain until I could form an actual plan in my mind. The thing was, Caer's prophecy hadn't been particularly helpful after all. Sure, it was well and good for me to accept all my past selves, but then what? I would have appreciated it if she'd spelled the whole thing out for me.

Nemain cocked her head. "I'm listening."

"My powers are all over the place. I think it has to do with remembering."

She swore beneath her breath. "I knew it."

"The two things are linked," I continued quickly. "The smiter's role and the remembering. I could explain it..."

"Yes, go on then," she snapped. "Hurry it up."

"If you let Tiarnan go."

"Clark, no," Tiarnan let out a low shout. "I'm not going to let you face this alone."

Nemain's eyes widened, and she let out a low chuckle. Her hand tightened around my arm again, and she pulled me close, hissing spit-filled words into my face. "You take me for some kind of fool, like I've never gone up against a Morrigan before. I see exactly what you're doing. There's no secret remembering, no link to your precious smiter. You just want me to let him out of his little cage so that the fight is two versus one. That's not going to happen, Clark. You want to fight me? You'll have to take me on your own."

29

Nemain let go of my arm and pushed hard against my shoulders. I stumbled back, eyes wide. That wasn't exactly what I'd expected to happen. I'd genuinely been trying to get Tiarnan out of this hellhole, not come up with some kind of fighting team. Though, now that I thought of it, it wouldn't have been a terrible idea.

Not that Nemain would have fallen for it.

She whipped a hidden knife from the back of her waistband and grinned. "This is what you wanted, right? A chance to take me down before your life is over forever? Well, here you are. One on one. You and me and no one else."

I bent my knees and raised my fists before me. "If you get a weapon, I should, too."

"Uh, uh." She wagged her finger. "You're the Morrigan. You're supposed to have more power in your pinky than all of us combined. Of course, I still managed to kill you. Not once but twice."

Okay, guys. Now would be a great time to say something,

don't you think? How do I fight her? But more importantly, how the hell do I win?

Silence reigned supreme.

With a frustrated grunt, I jumped sideways as she slashed her knife at my stomach. She let out a laugh when the blade came within inches of my skin.

"Not bad," she said, hopping back and forth on her feet. Her eyes were wild, the irises rimmed in red. "Truth be told, I didn't think you'd survive past the first slice."

"Clark," Tiarnan called out. "Remember your training. With *Balor*."

The emphasis on his name caught me off guard. I dodged another blow and sunk low to my knees. Calling upon my anger, white hot heat flooded through my veins. I screamed and slammed my hands onto the ground.

When I looked up, Nemain still stood tall. "Doesn't work on me. It never has. Nice try though."

Dammit, Morrigans. Give me something I can use.

In the back of my mind, something clicked. It wasn't a voice or a scream or a shout. It was me, my mind fitting jagged puzzle pieces together. My last dream had been illuminating, and now it flared up in my head as fresh and real as an actual memory. Nemain had pointed out two things. First, my past selves always forgot each other, and it made every single one of them weak. Second, when my magic mixed with Balor's...we were unstoppable. Our past lives had come together time and time again. Sometimes, it was love. Sometimes, it was war. But it had always been powerful.

Balor had also been scouring the grounds when I'd

INNOCENT UNTIL PROVEN FAE

been caught. I found it hard to believe that he would stop searching when he discovered I was gone. Which begged the question...where the hell was he now?

I bounced back and forth on my feet and narrowed my eyes. "You know, I could do this all day long. All I need is to buy Balor some time so he can storm in here and rescue me."

Nemain snorted and rolled her eyes. "You are so delusional. And talk about being the worst Morrigan I have ever met. Playing damsel in distress. I wish the others could see you now. They'd want to kick you in the teeth."

A slight prickle went across the back of my neck. Nemain was dead wrong. I didn't know it because of their voices whispering in my mind. I knew it because, somehow, deep down inside, I'd realised that we had become one. I no longer heard their voices. They weren't speaking to me. They didn't have to tell me what to do anymore because *they were me*.

"*I* am the Morrigan."

A flicker of doubt went through Nemain's eyes. "The Morrigan would never want a Prince to rescue her. Besides, he's not coming, little pretender. I caught him, same as I caught you. He's waiting his turn to be sacrificed, but I think we might save him for next week."

Ah, so there it was. The information I'd been hoping she'd spill. Balor was down here in the dungeons with me. He might be rooms away, but that was close enough. All I needed was just to find a tendril of his power. I would wrap it tightly around me, breathe it deep into my lungs.

I made a half-hearted effort to run at Nemain. She

JENNA WOLFHART

jumped out of the way easily enough, and tried her own blow in return. My mind was barely in it as I turned my mind outward. I'd never been able to read Balor, not unless he let me or his defences slipped for a tiny moment in time. But I would be able to feel him if I looked hard enough. His power, that intense magic that shook me to my very core.

A part of my soul sneaked away from the fight as I dodged and punched the air. It wound its way through the dungeons, reaching out this way and that with timid fingers. After what felt like hours, a strange electric power pulsed against my soul.

And so I gave it a push.

It pushed back, sneaking around me and squeezing tight.

A flush crept up my neck at the contact. Balor's presence sent my head spinning even when he wasn't in the same damn room. I focused on that feeling, on the intense need that washed over me. Our mating bond cinched tight, making my breath catch.

Nemain frowned and lowered her knife. "What the hell are you doing?"

"That's it, Clark," Tiarnan said. "Keep focusing on him."

Nemain whirled toward Tiarnan. "No one said you could speak, Fianna."

While Nemain had been twisted toward my fellow fae, a dark storm-cloud had taken shape across the stone floor. For once, I didn't push it away. Instead, I welcomed it with open arms. I thought about Balor, his hands on my skin, his lips on mine, how my core clenched tight when he caressed my hips.

Nemain stumbled back, shaking her head. "You

INNOCENT UNTIL PROVEN FAE

shouldn't be able to do this. The Morrigan has never had this kind of power before."

"Not alone, she hasn't." Pupils dilated, I strode toward her, arms outstretched. "You said it once before. Balor and I are stronger together than apart."

Confusion flickered across her face, but we were done with talking now. Tendrils of smoke curled from my open palms and shot toward Nemain. They wrapped tightly around her arms and legs, squeezing so tight a sharp cry exploded from her open mouth.

Nemain fought against the shadows that caressed her wrists. She kicked and pulled and ripped. But *we* kept our gaze focused hard, *our* emotions so tethered to the magic that nothing else existed in this world. Darkness filled *us* up with hate and pain.

This fae had been the end of *us*.

This fae had killed *us*.

We could never let her touch another fae again.

"Clark," Tiarnan called out, his voice breaking through the dark clouds churning through my mind. "We can just put her in a cage and lock her up. You don't have to take it any further than that."

Through gritted teeth, I said, "As long as she's alive, her bond controls every single fae in this Court. This is the only way to stop her."

"You're not a killer, Clark," he whispered.

"I'm not Clark." I yanked my hand, tightening the black bonds around Nemain's throat. "I am the Morrigan."

But then Nemain vanished, right into the very darkness itself. She was gone.

30

I strode up to the throne of skulls and perched on the edge. It felt strange, approaching it as the owner and not as a subject of the Court. The curving bones didn't feel right to me. The bumps meant I would never be able to lean back and relax. Maybe that was the point.

Balor watched me attempt to settle in to my new station, eyes dark and full of worry. "You don't seem happy."

I sighed. "How could I be? I had Nemain right in my grasp, and I somehow let her get away from me."

"Elena used the spell on Jake first, so that Nemain could consume his soul. She hadn't had enough time to practice his skill set yet, but she managed something in the end. Invisibility."

I nodded absently.

"You think those cells will hold Elena? A sorcerer with that kind of power?" I asked.

Balor pursed his lips. "It'll hold her for now. We might have to rethink things in the future."

JENNA WOLFHART

I nodded absently and glanced around the empty throne room. "They're still bonded to her. They have no idea what to do with themselves. Half of them think they need to fight me. The other half...they don't even want me near the throne, Balor. I only joined the Court a few months ago. They don't understand why they should follow me."

"They'll understand in time," he said quietly. "When they see exactly who and what you are."

We hadn't yet filled the Court in on my past lives as the Morrigan. At the moment, it was dangerous information. Their hearts and souls wanted to step forward and walk back into the life they'd once lived, but their minds stopped them, too controlled by Nemain's all-encompassing orders.

I didn't know what had happened to me down in the dungeons. Things had gotten kind of dark. Truth was, Dark Clark had been right. The last thing I wanted to do was take someone's life, but Nemain would always be a threat as long as she was alive.

She would return. And it wouldn't be long. What she would try next, no one knew. Her army could be in the dozens by then, but it could also be in the thousands. She had her sights set on Courts abroad.

Nemain had spent her entire life with one goal and one goal only: take my power and control the world. I might have gotten one up on her for the first time in her life, but it wouldn't happen again.

Balor knelt down before me and took my hand in his. "Are you okay after what happened in the dungeons? I know this strange magic between us worries you."

"I'm okay." I squeezed his hand. "As long as the dice land right."

He gave me a troubled smile.

I thought back to Nemain's words. "You were right, you know. In our past lives, we have always been linked. Sometimes love. Sometimes war. I feel like this life doesn't know quite what to do with us yet. After everything that happened with your sister and my parents, it's as if the magic was setting us up to be enemies this time around."

A deep frown stretched across Balor's face. "You can't mean that."

"Think about it, Balor. Everything in the world tried to make us hate each other." I leaned forward and pressed my forehead against his. "But then we met and the love came bursting through. Like an unstoppable force, even against the magic. But then we argue. We make up. We argue. We make up. It's like the dice is still spinning through the air. Will it land on love? Or will it land on war?"

"Love," Balor whispered fiercely. "It's already landed on love."

∾

Thank you for reading *Innocent Until Proven Fae*! The sixth and final book in the Paranormal PI Files, *All's Fae in Love and War*, will be launching at the end of September. You can sign up to my reader newsletter to be notified on release day.

ABOUT THE AUTHOR

Jenna Wolfhart is a Buffy-wannabe who lives vicariously through the kick-ass heroines in urban fantasy. After completing a PhD in Librarianship, she became a full-time author and now spends her days typing the fantastical stories in her head. When she's not writing, she loves to stargaze, rewatch Game of Thrones, and drink copious amounts of coffee.

Born and raised in America, Jenna now lives in England with her husband, her dog, and her mischief of rats.

FIND ME ONLINE
Facebook Reader Group
Instagram
YouTube
Twitter

www.jennawolfhart.com
jenna@jennawolfhart.com

Printed in Great Britain
by Amazon